"Where  sa?"

She didn't c [illegible] as a whisper. "Pl [illegible]

Didn't she care enough to explain? Had five months changed everything between them?

"I was worried, Marissa. I hired a private investigator when I couldn't find you myself. I was sure you'd phone or write, but I never heard a word. Where did you go? Why didn't you contact me?"

She turned her head to the wall, stared at the blinds that someone had opened to the morning sun.

"Aren't you going to answer me?" Gray asked his wife.

"Certainly. But I have a question, too."

"What is your question?"

"Would you mind telling me exactly who you are?"

Books by Lois Richer

Love Inspired

A Will and a Wedding #8
†*Faithfully Yours* #15
†*A Hopeful Heart* #23
†*Sweet Charity* #32
A Home, a Heart, a Husband #50
This Child of Mine #59
Baby on the Way #73
Daddy on the Way #79
Wedding on the Way #85
‡*Mother's Day Miracle* #101
‡*His Answered Prayer* #115
‡*Blessed Baby* #152
Tucker's Bride #182
Inner Harbor #207
***Blessings* #226
***A Time To Remember* #256

†Faith, Hope & Charity
*Brides of the Seasons
‡If Wishes Were Weddings
**Blessings in Disguise

LOIS RICHER

Sneaking a flashlight under the blankets, hiding in a thicket of Caragana bushes where no one could see, pushing books into socks to take to camp—those are just some of the things Lois Richer freely admits to in her pursuit of the written word. "I'm a bookaholic. I can't do without stories," she confesses. "It's always been that way."

Her love of language evolved into writing her own stories. Today her passion is to create tales of personal struggle that lead to triumph over life's rocky road. For Lois, a happy ending is essential.

"In my stories, as in my own life, God has a way of making all things beautiful. Writing a love story is my way of reinforcing my faith in His ultimate goodness toward us—His precious children."

A Time To Remember

Lois Richer

Published by Steeple Hill Books™

STEEPLE HILL BOOKS

ISBN 0-373-87266-6

A TIME TO REMEMBER

This edition published by arrangement with Steeple Hill Books.

www.SteepleHill.com

Printed in U.S.A.

We are saved by trusting.
And trusting means looking forward to getting something we don't yet have—for a man who already has something doesn't need to hope and trust that he will get it. But if we must keep trusting God for something that hasn't happened yet, it teaches us to wait patiently and confidently.

—*Romans* 8:24-25.

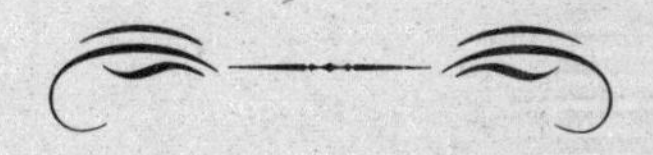

This book is offered, with love, to the Father.

Chapter One

Gaunt, eerie shadows quivered through the forest. Overhead the pines swayed in the night wind, the long needles of their swooping boughs brushing like feathers against her skin as she clawed her way through them, searching desperately for a way out.

She didn't know where she was. She didn't know if danger was behind or if it lurked ahead, waiting to trap her, to keep her from Cody. She only knew she had to keep going, had to press on, had to find her son. She knew she hadn't eased his fears when she'd told him she'd be back. There had been no time. She'd had to make him understand that they would get only one chance to escape. He must obey when she told him to run.

And run he had! He'd pressed through the forest, legs churning like windmills as he bounced along beside her without saying a word.

Their captor slept. But who knew for how long? They had to make a run for it now, while they could.

She had to get Cody out, get him back to Gray. Only then would her son be safe. Gray would protect Cody with his life.

Marissa had long since lost track of the days. But she knew the seasons were changing. The shorter days meant the warmth of the sun in the mornings had diminished. The river water felt chilly now, when such a short time ago it had seemed refreshing. If they didn't get away before winter set in, she didn't want to calculate their chances of reaching freedom. *He* had become too protective, too fixated. Her promises no longer satisfied him.

Now, as she ran through the bush, she prayed Cody was safe. She'd had to leave him, to detour around and disguise their tracks. Their abductor knew the bush, knew how to track. She knew very little, only that she had to make it as difficult for him to find them as she could.

Lord, she was tired.

Marissa leaned against a tree and fought to regain her breath. If only she could ask Gray what to do, if only she could borrow some of his strength. Gray. What must he think of her now? No calls, no letter, nothing. At least, she assumed there'd been no message to him. Maybe he thought she'd run away.

That last argument—no! He hadn't meant it. She knew he hadn't. It had been anger speaking, an outpouring of frustration.

Had he searched for her? And if he had, why hadn't he found them? Was it so easy for people to hide, even in this civilized world?

An owl hooted. She glimpsed its profile in the clearing just beyond.

Clearing? What had she done? Was she back where she'd begun?

"Oh, Father, I need help. Please show me the way. Get me to safety."

She glanced around, saw a figure slip stealthily across the clearing below. The full moon caught the silent glimmer of steel.

That knife! He was so good with it. She smothered a gasp of fear.

She'd tried to escape once before. The warning still rang in her ears. Try again and the boy would stay—without his mother. That's what scared her most. Cody growing up alone, without her or Gray. She had to get away.

Fear sent waves of panic rippling through her tired muscles. She'd run so far, tried so hard to cover their tracks. Would she stop now?

No.

The figure passed within inches of her, but Marissa shrank into the cover of overhanging boughs and remained hidden, scarcely breathing when he passed in front of her, sniffing the wind as if he knew she was nearby. At last it seemed safe. She eased out of her hiding place and tried to remember the direction she'd come before. But every path looked familiar. There was nothing to do but choose one and keep going.

And pray.

An hour later she admitted she was lost. Two hours later she'd passed her prison for the second time. Why hadn't she marked the way? What if Cody was discovered? Defeat dragged at her, but she refused to give up.

"Help me now, God. Lead me to safety, to Cody and home to Gray."

She opened her eyes, spied the moonbeams that lit up a small passage through the most dense area of the forest. If she went in there, she might never get out. But what other choice was there?

"'The Lord is my shepherd, I shall not want,'" she recited silently. "'He leadeth me beside the still waters. He restoreth my soul.'" She kept walking, kept reciting with no idea of time except for the path of the moon, which led her onward.

A sound caused her to pause. She whirled, saw the figure behind her and ran as hard as she could down through the ravine, then scrambled up the other side. She dug her fingers into the earth, uncaring that the rough branches and stones tore at her hands, that the sharp needles of pine and spruce stung her face.

"You took him. You took Brett away from me. You shouldn't have done that. Brett belongs to me. To me!"

Marissa tried to ignore the shrill screech. Was she closer now? She fought to gain a foothold in the mossy bank, forced her weary body to keep going.

"You have to be punished." The voice came from right behind her.

Her feet were sliding and she couldn't stop them. She reached out, grabbed something, heard an ominous crack above her.

He'd found her.

"Help me, God."

Pain exploded inside her head and she knew no more.

* * *

Five months, two days, eighteen hours. That's how long he'd been mired in this pit of suffering.

Gray McGonigle glanced around the cheerful kitchen his wife had taken such pleasure in decorating and felt his heart shrivel a little more. Would she ever come back, ever pull one of her pineapple upside-down cakes from the oven and tease him about his appetite?

And Cody—where was his son? Gray had promised God long before Cody was even born that he'd be the best father he could be as long as God kept Cody from the homeless life Gray had known as a child. So what had happened? Had he messed up? Was this God's revenge—to take both his wife and child?

Something inside him screamed, "No," but after five long months with few clues to their disappearance, Gray was so confused he didn't know what else to think. He knew Marissa. She wouldn't just take their son and disappear, not without telling him. Would she?

Maybe he didn't know her as well as he thought.

Disgusted with himself and the ever-present clouds of doubt, he surged to his feet. His body ached for repose, but his mind wouldn't stop asking questions to which there were no answers.

No one knew why Marissa had left, so how could Gray know if she would ever come back?

The phone pealed its summons into the silent room. He debated answering it, certain it would be Adam again, asking for money. His half brother had made no bones about his dislike of Gray or his disgust of their father's will, which had cut him out of the ownership of the ranch. Gray had no desire to go over it all again. But the phone wouldn't quiet, and finally he grabbed the receiver just to shut off the noise.

"Yeah?"

"Gray? Is that you?"

Not the baker woman! Dear Lord, he didn't want to listen to another of her little pep talks tonight.

"Gray?"

He was about to snap a response, then hesitated. Something in her voice told him she was upset. And Winifred Blessing seldom got upset about anything life threw at her.

"What's wrong, Miss Blessing?" Maybe focusing on someone else's problems would help him forget his own.

"Gray, we—we found Cody. Bless the Lord, we found Cody."

The words sucker punched him. His knees gave out and he collapsed onto a chair.

"Cody?" he squeaked, afraid to believe.

"He's all right, dear. A little scratched and bruised, but he seems fine. Luc's checking him out, just to be sure."

Gray had to ask.

"Marissa?"

"We're organizing a search party as we speak. Too bad it gets dark so early now, but we won't let a little September dusk stop us. She wouldn't have let Cody out of her sight, Gray. You know that."

Miss Winifred was solid bedrock. But just now he thought he'd heard a wobble in her voice. A second later it was gone, replaced by the firm conviction that had stood her through more than six decades of life.

"She's out there, I know it. We'll find her. You just hang on to your faith, Grayson. Can you do that?"

Gray figured his faith had died about four months ago when he'd heard nothing from his wife and son in a month, had gained no information from the man he'd hired to find them. But he wouldn't look back. Cody was home.

"Where are you, Miss Winifred?"

"In town, in the parking lot by the church. Can you come?"

"Try and stop me." He was out of the house and barreling down the road thirty seconds later, his heart pumping like a jackhammer. "Come on, Marissa," he muttered, peering into the gloom of an autumn evening. "Come home to me. Please come home."

He couldn't pray. God had betrayed him with the two things entrusted to him. How could he trust again? Now it was time for him to take control. It was his job to take care of his wife and son, and he'd do it, no matter what.

At the far side of the church parking lot a small crowd had gathered. Gray raced across the pavement, pushed his way through, his mind screaming his son's name. He jerked to a halt at the heart-stopping sight of his boy seated in Miss Winifred's lap, munching on a cookie he held in one hand. The fingers of the other were closed around the small glass figurine that had disappeared with him, a gift from the grandfather he'd barely known.

"Cody?"

At his whisper, the boy glanced up, grinned and jumped to his feet. Gray scooped the beloved wriggling body into his arms and held on as hard as he could. Tears obscured the landscape, blurred his vision, but it didn't matter that the whole town would see him bawling. Cody was home. Cody was safe. For now he'd let himself revel in that.

''Gray?'' Luc Lawrence stood at his elbow, his eyes dark with concern. ''Can you give him to Dani? Just for a moment? We need to talk.''

Gray's fingers tightened. He pressed Cody away just enough to stare into his tear-filled eyes, glimpsed the receding terror. Scrapes, bruises—yes, he had lots of those. But he looked fine. He looked wonderful.

''There'll be time to talk later,'' he told Luc, speaking past the lump lodged in his throat. ''For now just let me hold my son.'' He hugged the little boy close, wallowing in the feel of those precious pudgy fingers against his face. ''Are you okay, Cody? Are you all right?'' He tilted back, searched the eyes Marissa claimed were mirror copies of his own.

''Where's Mommy, Cody? What happened to Mommy?''

Big fat tears coursed down Cody's dirty cheeks as he stared at his dad.

''You can tell me, son. I just want to help. I won't be mad. Honest. Tell Daddy where Mommy is.''

''Gray, please, will you just listen to me?'' Luc dragged at his arm, but Gray jerked away.

''Leave us alone, Luc,'' he snarled. ''This is my son, my only son. If he has any idea where Marissa is, he's got to tell us.'' He smoothed a hand over Cody's head. ''Where's Mommy, son?''

''Gray, he can't tell you that.''

''What?'' Gray stared at the town's newest doctor, then glanced over at Joshua and Nicole Darling, seeking answers to questions he didn't want to ask. His fingers tightened around the precious body pressed to his chest. "What are you talking about? Why can't he tell me? Has something—"

"We don't know where Marissa is yet. We're still looking. Once the sheriff came, did his thing, the whole town showed up. They're searching the ravine right now." Dr. Nicole Darling's eyes warned him to follow her lead. She stepped forward, placed her hand on Cody's arm. "Cody, can you stay with Miss Winifred while I talk to your daddy for a minute? I promise it won't take long. You can stand right here beside her and watch us, if you like. Okay?"

Misty silver eyes, too serious for a child his age, studied Gray for interminable minutes. Finally Cody nodded, pressed himself away from his father, struggled to get down, fingers white as he squeezed the horse he held. Gray let him go, barely stemming his need to grab him and hang on for all he was worth. Cody walked over beside Miss Winifred and thrust his hand into hers, but he kept his eyes on his father.

"Okay, something's going on. What is it?" He glanced at the three doctors in turn and knew the news wouldn't be good. "Spill it. Did something happen to Cody? Is he sick?"

"He won't speak, Gray. We don't know what happened to him, but we think something traumatized him badly enough to stop his speech." Joshua Darling, the senior partner in Blessing's medical practice, put a hand on his shoulder and kept it there, his voice low but firm. "There's a technical name for this, which I know you don't care about. The gist of the diagnosis is that Cody's problem doesn't seem to be medical—

there's no sign of injury. Though we don't know why, we think he's unconsciously decided that he's not going to speak. Not yet, anyway."

"Can you accept that?" Luc demanded.

"I—I don't know." Not speak? For how long? Cody, the boy who had always brimmed with giggles just begging to be free—that beloved voice silent?

What could have happened to do this to my child?

Gray wanted to hit something. Images he'd seen on the street when he was not much older than Cody rifled through his mind. What horror had his child observed? If he didn't talk about them, didn't let Gray help, how would they ever be able to erase those pictures? Then Gray remembered—he hadn't yet forgotten the images from his own childhood, and he was a lot older than Cody.

Fear loomed large in Gray's mind.

"How long will this not speaking last?"

"We don't know. Tomorrow morning I'll phone a specialist and Cody can see him. We'll find out exactly what's going on. But tonight I've told the police I think it's best if you just let him get used to being back home. Don't ask questions, don't push him, don't press for more than he's ready to give. Most of all, don't ask him about Marissa. Apparently it scares him." Joshua frowned. "Can you do it? Because if you can't let go of all the questions and just let him relax, I'm going to check him in to the hospital."

"What's wrong—"

Joshua shook his head.

"I checked him over. So did Luc. We can't find anything wrong. The damage seems to be psychological, and even that may only be temporary."

''The thing is, Gray,'' Luc murmured, laying one hand on his arm, ''he's obviously gone through some sort of ordeal. But right now the details aren't important.''

Gray snorted. ''Of course they're important. Marissa could be holed up somewhere against her will. We've got to find her.''

''Listen to me.'' Luc lowered his voice, his look intent as he focused on Gray. ''We don't know about Marissa. You have to face it. We don't know if she's alive or dead. Not yet. But we know Cody is here. He needs you. You must focus on his needs right now. The police will find your wife and the perpetrator, but at this moment your place is with your son.''

''Marissa would never have let him go without a fight.'' Gray's confidence would not be shaken. ''If it was possible, she would have followed him.''

''I know. We all believe she's out there somewhere.'' Nicole tried to soften the pain with her sympathetic words. ''But maybe she's hurt. A thousand things could have happened to her. There's no point in conjecturing. Right now you've got to focus on Cody.''

She was right. Though his heart ached with loss for Marissa, though he wanted to tear up the countryside, find her and never let her go—right now one thing took precedence. Cody. Marissa would want him to concentrate on their son, to do what she couldn't. Maybe never would.

No! He wouldn't think like that. She was all right. She had to be.

All Gray knew right now was that he couldn't lose

this second chance to be the kind of father he knew he could be.

God wouldn't fault him a second time.

He stood in the shade of the pine tree and stared down at her, scared by the trail of blood that trickled from her head. Blood was bad.

"You shouldn't have run," he whispered, angry that she hadn't obeyed. "I told you not to run. That was very bad. Now you're hurt and there's no one to make you better." He put his knife back in the leather holder strapped to his belt and waited for her to tell him what she'd done with Brett.

But she didn't wake up. Not for a long time.

And then there were voices, people calling.

They were looking for her. If she woke up now, she'd run away again. Maybe she wouldn't wake up, maybe they wouldn't find her and he would learn where she'd taken Brett. He glanced down, saw the dirty shoes. If she couldn't run, she couldn't get away. He slipped them off her feet, tucked them into his belt.

The voices were coming closer.

He shimmied up the nearest tree, hid himself among the thick branches and waited. After a while some people saw her and rushed over to help her. Still she didn't wake up.

"Look at this! Someone hit her with it." A man in a police uniform held up a branch with blood on it. "Don't move her. I'll radio for a stretcher. Maybe one of the doctors will want to look at her first."

He was scared now. He hadn't hit her. He wasn't bad. He wanted to tell them that. But they wouldn't understand. Nobody understood about Brett. That's why he'd run away.

So he sat in his tree and waited some more.

After a while he grew tired of sitting above them, watching in the tree. But there was no way to get down without being seen. Besides, maybe these people knew where she'd taken Brett. He'd have to stay still and listen.

So he waited some more.

"At least she got the boy to safety. Now he's with his father, he'll be okay."

"I don't know about that. I heard he won't talk."

Brett wouldn't talk? He leaned down, trying to hear more.

"You mean he couldn't tell them what happened?"

"Nope. Didn't say a word."

He smiled, nodded. That was his friend, his very best friend, Brett.

Brett wouldn't tell them. Brett loved him. And he loved Brett. He'd just have to find him and bring him back. This time *she* couldn't come. She didn't belong.

He waited. More people came. Finally they carried her away. He waited and listened and watched, and when there wasn't a sound in the forest, he slipped out of his hiding place and hurried back to the special place. It was pitch-black, but he needed no flashlight. He knew the way like the back of his hand. As he walked, he thought about what to do next.

Brett was with his daddy.

He remembered their talks, remembered about the horses and the long road and the big house.

He'd go back into town, listen to what the people said.

And then he'd find Brett and bring him back.

They belonged together.

Chapter Two

In the soft butter sun of midmorning Gray picked up the receiver.

"Hello?"

"It's good news, Gray. We found her. In the ravine. Her clothes are tattered and torn, her body is a mass of cuts and bruises, but she's alive."

"What aren't you saying?" Gray knew there was more. He could feel the tingles of apprehension winging over the airwaves.

"Right now she's unconscious. Marissa has a head injury, Gray, and a pretty good-sized cut. I put in seventeen stitches." Luc's voice relayed his concern. "I think you'd better pray, buddy."

Pray? Ask God again, when He hadn't answered last time?

He pushed the frustration aside, concentrated on the words. Gray frowned.

"You're saying she fell and hit her head?"

"Or was struck—from behind. The police found a bloody branch."

"He followed her?" It was a nightmare from which he couldn't seem to waken. "Why? He never took her money from the car. That was left inside, with her purse. At least, that's what the sheriff said."

"I don't know why someone would have hit her. Maybe this guy's a wacko. Maybe he wanted something else. We've given her a full examination, ordered scans, the whole bit. The main thing for you to remember is that she's back."

"I'll come right away."

"No, let Cody sleep. I promise I'll phone as soon as she wakes."

"You do that. Get her anything she needs, Luc. Anything. It doesn't matter how much it costs." He couldn't say any more for the blockage in his throat.

"You know I'll take care of her, man. Depend on it." Luc's voice was filled with promise. "How's your son?"

"Cody hasn't slept all night. His eyes close and he almost lets go, but then something jerks him awake. I've been watching him. Maybe he needs a shot or something?" Never in his life had Gray felt so helpless, so out of control.

"No, I'd rather not sedate him. Let him get through this on his own first. Later, if he needs something, we'll administer it, but until we know more, I think he's better to get reacquainted with his dad in his own way."

"Yeah, okay. Thanks, Luc."

"My pleasure, man. My pleasure. I'm just glad they're home."

"Yeah." Gray hung up, caught sight of Cody standing in the doorway and beckoned.

Cody raced over, then stopped. He glanced at the phone, frowned his question.

"That was Dr. Luc. Remember him?"

Cody nodded, one eyebrow quirked upward.

"He phoned to tell us that they found your mom. She hurt her head and they've taken her to the hospital for tests, so we can't see her right now. But once the doctors fix her up, she'll be fine." *I hope.*

Cody stared at him, his confusion evident.

"Mommy's going to get all better, Cody. Do you understand?"

Tears dripped from the little boy's tanned cheeks, but his gray eyes shone like hammered silver when Cody finally nodded his comprehension.

"Right now I think you'd better get some sleep. Okay, son?"

Cody shook his head, adamantly refusing.

"You're not tired? Well, do you want some breakfast?"

Cody shook his head again.

Well, what then? There must be something a father could do for his kid. Gray studied the beloved face for several moments before understanding dawned.

"You want to go see Mommy?"

Cody grinned.

"Okay, sport, we'll go. But I don't know what you're going to wear. You've grown about three inches. I don't think any of your old stuff will fit."

Cody grabbed his hand and dragged him toward the stairs up to his room.

"Yeah, you're right. We'll find something. After

all, what do clothes matter when your mom's back? Let's go see Mommy."

Half an hour later as he drove back into town, Gray felt exactly the way Cody looked—hopeful, excited, a bit worried, unsure of himself. What would Marissa say? Would she be awake and able to tell him where she'd been? Could she identify her abductor? Would he finally have the answers he craved?

Most of all, would she accept his apology or throw it back in his face?

The hospital parking lot was almost empty. Gray pulled in as near to the entrance as he legally could. Cody hopped out before he could be helped, his eyes dancing with excitement, impatient to get inside.

"Come on, son. Let's go find her."

There was no one at the admissions desk, which wasn't surprising in their small-town hospital. Noises from a treatment room in the adjoining emergency ward helped Gray assume the nurse was busy there. It wasn't a large building. It wouldn't take long to find Marissa.

He spotted a sleeping Miss Winifred sitting on a lounge in one ward, head jerking forward in spasmodic nods. She awoke as soon as he approached.

"Hi, Gray. A friend of mine came in with chest pains last night. I was here when they brought Marissa back, so I thought I'd stay, catch forty winks and speak to her when she woke up. Hello, Cody. How are you today?"

Cody grinned at Miss Winifred, accepting her hug.

Back? Brought her back from where? Gray pushed that aside to mull over later. He didn't have time to puzzle it out right now. There were other things to consider. He glanced around, thinking about Luc's words. Maybe it would be better if he saw Marissa alone for the first time. If her injuries involved her face, Cody would need to be prepared. Personally, Gray didn't care what she looked like—he only wanted her in his arms. For the rest of his life.

"Cody, I'm going to find your mom. I want you to stay with Miss Winifred until I come and get you. We have to be very quiet so we don't wake up the sick people. Okay?"

Cody frowned, obviously wanting to argue, but Gray shook his head as he hunkered down in front of the boy.

"Don't worry, son. I'm not leaving you. I'll be back. I promise. I just need to see Mommy. I haven't seen her for such a long time and I missed her a lot. Just like I missed you. After I've talked to her a little while, I'll come back and get you. Okay?"

Cody was obviously debating, but Gray figured the boy was finding it hard to argue without speaking.

"Come on, Cody. I'll read you this story I found about a king." Miss Winifred winked at Gray, then continued speaking to the boy. "Your daddy just wants a minute to hug and kiss your mommy without you watching. It's mushy adult stuff. I don't think you want to watch that, do you?"

Cody looked at Gray as if he couldn't remember such a thing ever happening. But after a moment he nodded and reached inside his grubby jacket. Gray stared at the picture he'd scribbled on a wrinkled sheet of paper, his name carefully inscribed below.

When had he learned to write his name?

Gray bit his lip as the impact of the many things he'd missed these past five months hit home.

Cody held his gaze, his stare never wavering as he waited for his father to take the picture. There were trees, lots of them. And two figures. One small. One large. Behind the trees was a shadowy shape that Gray understood to identify their abductor. He stared at it for some clue that would unlock his son's silence. He found nothing.

He hunkered down, peered into his son's clear gaze. "It's a very nice picture, Cody," he murmured. "Do you want me to give it to Mommy?"

Cody nodded.

"Okay." He accepted the picture, held it carefully while Cody settled himself in Winifred's lap. "I'll go find her and give her your picture."

Satisfied that the boy was occupied and safe, Gray started down the hall. Outside the third door he heard a voice he hadn't heard in five long months. Gray shoved the door open and stepped inside.

"Is anyone there? Oh. Hello. Can you please get me some aspirin?"

"Hello, Marissa." He couldn't help staring, his eyes absorbing the damaged but still fragile beauty of her sculpted face, the deep rich sapphire of her eyes, the fair skin that never quite tanned so much as her freckles joined forces to give the illusion of sun-kissed skin.

The golden tumble of her beautiful hair lay matted against her scalp, her nape hidden beneath a thick bandage.

"Hello." She inspected him from head to toe. "You don't look the medical type. Would you mind finding a nurse? I've tried to get out of this bed and do it myself, but every time I push on these bed rails, my head starts whirling. If I could just get some aspirin, I'm sure this headache would ease.''

''I don't know if they'll allow you to have medication until they've done all the tests. You have a head injury, remember? But I can go look for someone.'' He surveyed her bruised face, broken nails and the scratches that covered her arms. ''You look like you fought a cougar,'' he muttered, his stomach clenching at the thought of what she must have been through.

''I feel like it, too.'' She eased her head back on the pillows and closed her eyes. ''Do you mind if we continue this discussion later? My head is about to shatter.''

''Yeah, sure. I guess.'' It stung that she brushed his concern off as if five months ago she'd simply driven to Denver for a day of shopping and he was nothing more than the parking attendant. ''Where have you been, Marissa?''

She didn't even open her eyes, but her voice was a whisper. ''Please leave me alone.''

Impotent rage burned deep inside. Didn't she care enough to even explain? Had five months changed everything between them? Was she remembering those last awful words he'd thrown at her?

''I was worried, Marissa. Scared stiff. I hired a private investigator when I couldn't find you myself. I was sure that you'd phone or write. Something. But I never heard a word from you or Cody. What happened?''

Her eyes were open now. She was staring at him as if he were a specimen she was trying to define. Her blue eyes had darkened until they were almost navy. With fear? Of him?

"What do you want from me?" she asked huskily.

"What do I want? I want answers." She was frail, she was hurt. But the need to know could not be stifled. "Where did you go, Marissa? What have you been doing? Why didn't you contact me?"

"Good questions."

"Well?"

She turned her head to the wall, stared at the blinds that someone had turned open to the morning sun. Gray waited, anger building inside. What was going on with her? Why was she acting like this?

"Aren't you even going to answer me?" he sputtered, clenching his hands at his sides.

"Certainly. In due time. But I have a question, too." She pleated the sheet with her left hand. "Perhaps you wouldn't mind answering that first?"

"I guess." He shrugged, pretending nonchalance when he knew she was going to ask about that day. "What is your question?"

"Would you mind telling me exactly who you are?"

Chapter Three

His eyes flashed like lightning, changing from a soft dove-gray to hardened steel.

"I'm your husband."

She stared at him while her mind desperately tried to process the information. Husband? She had a husband? Wouldn't a woman remember if she had a husband?

"Gray," he prompted, frowning at her. "Gray McGonigle."

"And I'm Marissa McGonigle. I see." She couldn't blame him for his belligerent tone. It seemed perfectly understandable now. "I was your wife. I was married to you."

"*Are* married to me," he corrected, his tone belligerent. "Unless something's happened that I don't know about. Do you remember?"

She hated to destroy that sad-eyed look of puppy-dog hope in his eyes, but she couldn't pretend. Not about this.

"I'm sorry. I don't remember anything." Marissa. She turned the name over in her mind. She liked it. It sounded different, special. As if someone had taken the time to choose a name specifically for her. "My parents?" she asked, suddenly wondering why only he was here.

"Both dead. Your father died when you were little. Your mother died two years ago. Breast cancer."

"Oh." She felt flat, deflated, as if she'd unconsciously expected—what? Someone to be there? She chided herself for her silliness. Who else did she want? Wasn't an unknown husband enough?

"What *do* you remember, Marissa?" He squinted at her as if he thought she was playing some childish game.

She attributed the angry frustration in his voice to worry. He must be worried. A husband would be worried if his own wife didn't recognize him. Wouldn't he?

But this man didn't look frazzled or afraid. Or worried. He looked…defeated, she decided after a moment's contemplation. As if he'd tried very hard and just couldn't manage to make sense of his world.

She scoured her brain for something, some ray of hope she could offer. To her shock, nothing emerged. She looked at the gold band on his ring finger, then at the matching circlet guarded by a blazing diamond on her own left hand, and suddenly realized that she didn't know how it got there.

"Nothing," she whispered. "I remember nothing." She stared at him. Blank. Her heart picked up speed as she peered around the room, stared out the window, squinted at the picture he'd laid on top of her blanket. ''What's this?''

''A picture. Cody made.''

''That's nice.'' Whoever Cody was. ''Will you thank him for me?'' She stared at the childish scribbles, smiled at the ghostly figure fluttering among the trees. ''Is it almost Halloween?''

''No. That's about seven weeks away.'' His dark brows joined to hood his eyes. ''Why?''

She shrugged. ''It looks like a Halloween picture, that's all. I'll bet he's a cute kid.''

''Yes.'' The man named Gray nodded. ''Our son is a wonderful boy. But he's got some problems, I'm afraid.''

Whatever else he said slid past in a whirl of confusion. She got stuck on those words *our son.*

''Cody is my child?'' she gasped.

''Well, he's both of ours,'' he agreed, one corner of his mouth tilting up in a half smile. ''You used to say he got all my genes, but I'm pretty sure his stubbornness came from you.''

''A child.'' She laid a hand against her abdomen as if that might somehow reawaken slumbering memories of pregnancy, labor, delivery. ''How old is he?''

''Five. Almost six.'' He sighed, slumped against the wall and raked a hand through his hair. ''I'm guessing you don't remember him, either.''

Marissa shook her head, then stopped the action immediately as pain threatened to swamp her tired aching body.

''I'm sorry,'' she whispered, tears welling for all the precious memories she couldn't share with him. And she wanted to. Something about this man drew her soul, called to her. Surely somewhere in her brain she knew him?

Yet her brain drew a blank.

"It's not your fault."

But he sounded as if he thought it was.

"I suppose I should be grateful that my existence isn't the only thing you've managed to wipe from your mind."

Oh, the pain underlying those words. She could feel the despair gripping him, dragging him down. He'd obviously been up all night. A five-o'clock shadow gave him an edgy flair that only enhanced his harsh features. His cheekbones were definitely a legacy from his distant Cherokee heritage, but those lean, taut muscles and that burnished tan came from hard physical labor.

Marissa froze, tried to figure out how she'd come to that conclusion. But the mist that carried the insight had dissipated and she couldn't bring it back.

"Good morning, Marissa." A doctor who clearly knew her strode into the room, saw Gray and grinned. "You didn't waste any time getting here."

"No."

She sensed there was something else the man—her husband—wanted to say. But he clamped his lips together and thrust his hands into the pockets of his worn blue jeans.

The doctor was puzzled. He glanced from her to him, then shrugged.

"How are you feeling, Marissa?"

"She's got a headache. And she doesn't remember *anything*."

Marissa glared at Gray. Did he have to say it like

that, tacked on at the end as if she'd deliberately done it to spite him? Why did he always…what? The memory eluded her.

"I can speak for myself," she muttered, fighting to retain her composure.

Again that careless shrug, the slumping pose, the thrust of that granite chin. "So do it."

"Thank you. I will. If you'll let me." She wanted it clear up front that she wasn't going to turn into some kind of shrinking violet, no matter what she'd been like before.

The doctor ignored their verbal battle, eyes concerned as he swung his flashlight across her pupils, took her pulse, checked her reactions.

"What specifically don't you remember?" he asked gently, frowning at her tear-filled eyes. "Do you remember me? Luc Lawrence? I moved here just after Dr. Darling had his accident. Joshua Darling."

He could have been speaking Hindi for all she understood. Marissa frowned, waited for something. Nothing. No flash of comprehension, no lightning stroke of memory. Nothing.

"I'm married to Dani. You and Gray live next door to her ranch. Gray's renting the land."

"Oh." She leaned back against the pillow and wished it would all go away. It hurt too much to think. "How did I get here?" she asked a moment later.

"We were hoping you could tell us." Gray pushed away from the wall, his attention riveted on her, his eyes searching for—what? "You and Cody disappeared over five months ago. No one's been able to find out where you went or what you've been doing. Then last night Cody showed up in the church parking lot. He was bruised, a little roughed up. But he's fine.'' He stopped, watched her. ''Except that he won't talk.''

''Why?'' She felt sorry for the little boy, then realized she was thinking about her own son. ''I mean, what do you think happened?''

''We were hoping you could explain.'' Gray looked at the doctor. Something unspoken passed between them.

''Marissa, you were found about a mile down a very steep ravine, about half a mile away from where police think Cody crawled up. Do you recall that?'' The doctor's eyes were gentle, caring. They didn't demand answers, not like Gray's.

She frowned, closed her eyes, tried to imagine what she would have been doing in a ravine. Like a quilt, fear settled on her shoulders in a shroud she couldn't shake. Swirls of nebulous memories that couldn't be defined wavered behind her eyes. Only one word came to mind.

Run!

''Marissa! Marissa, it's okay. You're safe. Nothing will hurt you here.'' Dr. Luc's fingers squeezed her arms and at once the memories faded, the fear lifted.

''What just happened?'' Gray looked from the doctor to her, confusion evident.

''I think you had a flashback, didn't you?'' Luc murmured, holding her wrist as he measured her pulse. ''Can you tell us what you saw?''

''Not—not really.'' She shrank against the pillows at the sparks that lit Gray's eyes. ''I *can't!* It was just shadows and whispers, nothing I could explain. And fear. I felt fear. I had to run.'' She shivered, and her voice died away at the cold black terror of it.

''It's okay. You're safe.'' Gray's fingers, warm and strong, closed around hers. ''Anything else you can remember? Anything at all? A house, flowers? Did you follow a road? Anything?''

Because he looked so sad, she closed her eyes and waited for the black shroud to drown her. When it didn't, she sighed, felt his thumb rubbing against her wrist in a soothing caress that allowed her to relax and stop fighting the hammer in her head. A picture wavered before her mind.

''There's a river,'' she whispered. ''I'm swimming in a river.'' Then the picture was gone and she couldn't remember when or why or how she came to be in that river.

''That might not be a recent memory, Gray,'' she heard the doctor whisper. ''There's no way of knowing just where her mind selected that from. She might have been a child.''

''I wasn't a child,'' she insisted, eyes wide open, slightly insulted that they thought they could speak in front of her, as if she were deaf. ''I was like I am now.'' She frowned. ''No, wait a minute.'' Something wasn't right.

''It wasn't exactly swimming,'' she murmured, confused by the impressions she was feeling. ''But I was in the water up to my neck. It was cold, but it felt good.''

''Was Cody there? Can you picture Cody?''

She cast about, trying to home in on a picture of a little boy, but nothing came.

''I don't think so.'' Marissa opened her eyes, shrugged. ''I can't remember.''

Gray sighed, the light in his eyes fading. She saw Luc reach out, touch his shoulder.

''Maybe it's a nightmare, Luc,'' her husband offered. ''Marissa never swims. She's afraid of the water. You wouldn't believe the lectures she's given me about water safety. When I took Cody fishing last year—''

She felt his hands tighten against hers before he drew them away, the sentence dying on his lips just as the hope flickered out of his eyes.

''Bubbles.'' The word popped out of her without any conscious thought.

''What?''

Both men stared at her as if she were insane. Then Gray looked to Luc for direction. But the doctor was intent on his own thoughts.

''Bubbles,'' she repeated, trying to understand what had prompted her to say it.

''You were washing.'' Luc looked from Gray to Marissa, his eyes sparkling with excitement. ''Don't you see? Soap. Bubbles. You were washing in the water.''

''Washing clothes?'' she asked doubtfully, searching for the thread of a memory that eluded her.

Luc shook his head.

''Yourself. You said you were up to your neck. You wouldn't go that deep to wash clothes, but you would if you were taking a bath.''

Gray stared at him, nodded. ''So wherever you were staying, it was beside water. And you were confined.'' He pointed to the marks on her wrists.

Marissa hadn't noticed them before, but now the

blue-tinged rings held her in a grip of fear. *Get away. Get away from here.*

The pain was suddenly excruciating and she whimpered as it flooded over her. Just from the corner of her eye she saw Gray glare at Luc, his eyes asking a question. Luc shook his head.

She closed her eyes, almost passing out as a new wave sucked her strength.

''Oh, please help me.'' The hand with the IV in it felt too heavy to lift, but she did it anyway, rubbing one finger against her forehead to ease the stabbing pressure.

''What's wrong, Marissa?''

''My head,'' she whispered. ''Please give me something to stop my head from hurting.''

''I'll help you, I promise,'' Luc murmured, checking her pupils again. ''You can go to sleep soon. But I want you to think for just one minute more.''

The pinpricks of light from his flashlight sent waves of nausea over her body, but Marissa fought back, sucked in deep breaths of air and forced herself to relax.

''Think about what?''

''Your head hurts because it has a cut on it. Do you remember how you got that cut?''

The black curtain was hanging there again, just waiting to drop down and shut out all the questions. In a way, that's what she wanted—oblivion. But the doctor's tone was so gentle, so soothing, she tried to answer him.

''I was running,'' she whispered. ''Running away.''

''From what?''

But the answer wasn't there. Instead, the black curtain whooshed down and Marissa couldn't answer.

"Did she faint? What's wrong with her?"

"Nothing. Her brain had enough poking and probing and it shut down. She seems fine. Her vital signs are all excellent. Her scans were clear. She responded to all the stimuli tests we performed. The specialist's report was faxed in this morning. Everything is normal."

"What specialist?" Gray growled the words, knowing he should be thanking Luc, not badgering him. But every time he thought of her tied up, trying to get away, his stomach knotted. He slammed his fist against his thigh in frustration.

"I had her airlifted to the city as soon as we found her." Luc's cheeks turned red, but he held Gray's stare. "I had to. I didn't know how long she'd been out or what we'd find and I wanted to know immediately if there was brain damage."

Gray winced, but kept his focus on Luc, pinning him.

"And you didn't phone me until after they'd brought her back, did you?"

"No."

"What if she'd died?"

Luc shook his head.

"Would God do that? Bring her home to let her die? I don't think so, buddy. Where's your faith?" He stepped backward when Gray surged forward, held up one hand. "Okay, okay. But just think about it. You had to concentrate on Cody. There was nothing you could do for Marissa. But I could, and I did."

''You decided this all on your own?'' Fury and indignation fought for supremacy. ''Who consented to her care?''

''You did, through me.'' Luc winced at his growl. ''The three of us, Joshua, Nicole and I, consulted and decided it was for the best. We couldn't let anything happen to Marissa, Gray. We just couldn't.''

Gray sighed. What was wrong with him?

''I know. I should be thanking you instead of acting like an outraged—''

''Husband?'' Luc grinned. ''But that's what you are. And I don't blame you.'' He picked up Marissa's slim, scratched hand, grazing the tip of his finger over her injuries. ''She put up quite a fight.''

Gray gulped, thrust away the images his brain conjured up. He could hardly bring himself to ask the next question, but he needed to know.

''You're sure she wasn't attacked?''

''Physically I believe she might have been,'' Luc told him quietly. ''But sexually?'' He shook his head. ''I did a full rape kit. There's no evidence of that.''

''Thank God.'' Gray sagged with relief.

''Indeed. You should be thanking Him for a lot of things, not the least of which is that your family has been restored to you. A little the worse for wear, perhaps, but they are back.''

''For now. But what's to stop this from happening again? Who abducted them? We still don't know that, Luc. And someone must have if her hands were tied.'' He reached out, fury raging inside as he traced the unmistakable marks of rope burns.

Luc clapped him on the shoulder.

''I know you'll probably tell me to mind my own

business, but I have to say it anyway. This is something you have to take to God. There's no other person who has the answers you want. You're going to have to ask Him to explain it to you.'' He turned, pulled open the door.

Gray stepped forward, grabbing his arm.

''Where are you going? Don't you have to watch her for complications?''

''Someone will be monitoring her, Gray. They'll keep me up to speed. Right now I've got rounds to do.'' Luc paused a moment, spared a glance for Marissa, then smiled. ''Besides, I'm sure you're the best company for your wife right now. Why don't you pull up a chair and just sit here for a while? I'm sure Marissa will have a thousand and one questions when she wakens.''

''Then you think she's going to regain her memory? All of it?'' Relief flooded him. One by one he loosened his fisted fingers. ''When?''

''That's not up to me, I'm afraid.'' Luc's rueful face gave away his feelings. ''But God has a plan, buddy. A good one. And He knows what He's doing. Leave it up to Him. Rest in His care.''

Gray didn't want to wait for anything. He was sick of the uncertainty, sick of waiting for the next disaster, afraid to learn what waited around the next corner. If he could, he'd gather Marissa up in his arms, find Cody and take both of them back to the safety he could provide at the ranch. Unfortunately, hiding wouldn't help either of them right now. Marissa needed medical care and Cody needed both of them.

''Did you hear me?'' Luc asked.

''Yeah, I heard,'' was all he could manage to say.

He stared at Marissa's still form and wondered if they'd ever regain the life they'd shared, if she'd ever look at him the way she once had. He didn't deserve it, not after what he'd said. But deep inside, away from the cynicism and anger, hope floated in a little round bubble.

Maybe, just maybe he hadn't lost everything he loved.

''And Gray?''

''Yeah?'' It hurt to look at her and know she felt nothing for him. Gray wheeled around, faced the doctor. ''What is it?''

''Cody needs to see her. He needs to touch her and know she's fine. Then I want him to see a psychologist.''

''Where?'' How in the world could he nurse an amnesiac wife, protect his little boy and run a ranch?

''Right here, today. Dr. Scallion is here for his weekly appointments. God evidently knew we'd need the guy, so He had him change his scheduled day in town from yesterday to today. And he's got lots of time to see Cody.''

''You're the doctor.''

''Yes, I am. Don't forget it.'' Luc's voice toughened to the gruff but tender tones Gray had heard him use on obstreperous patients. ''Don't tell me God hasn't protected those two, Gray McGonigle. I doubt if you'll ever know just how tenderly He cared for them when you couldn't.''

The door creaked shut behind him.

Gray walked back to the bed, stared at Marissa's bruised, battered face, and blood-covered hair, scratched arms. He recalled Cody's tortured look each time he tried to fall asleep. He remembered his own long days, and even longer nights when he'd stuffed his face in his pillow to stop from sobbing his heart out at their loss.

What kind of tender care was that? What kind of God did that?

Ten thousand times he'd asked the question, ten thousand times he'd come up blank. God, or at least what he knew of God, was supposed to be love. He was supposed to tenderly care for those who followed Him. Marissa wasn't perfect, but she sure didn't deserve to be kidnapped by some crazy person. He, on the other hand, probably deserved everything God had sent him, and then some. But why not punish him directly?

He directed his arguments heavenward, but there was no response and his frustration and impotence at the situation burgeoned.

Some time later the door creaked open and Cody peeked around the corner. Gray held out a hand, drew him into the room, smiling at the cookie crumbs on Cody's lips.

"I was just coming to get you. What have you been eating?"

Cody brought the little white box out from behind his back. He pointed to the delicate red script flowing across one corner. "Blessing Bakery—made with love."

A creation from Miss Winifred. Gray might have guessed. He smiled at the older woman, motioned her to come inside.

"We had breakfast quite a while ago, then Cody saw a nice doctor. After that we went for lunch. I had

Furley bring him over a little treat.'' Miss Winifred glanced at the bed, smiled, then looked at him. ''I don't think you realize how long you've been in here, Gray. It's almost two o'clock.''

He glanced at his watch, saw that she was right.

''I apologize, Miss Win. I've held you up from work. You've been wonderful to look after Cody like this, but he can stay with me now. Marissa woke up once when I first came in, but she's been asleep ever since. They tell me that's perfectly normal. That her body needs rest.''

''Yes, Luc told me, as well.'' She laid a hand on his shoulder. ''Are you all right, dear?''

''I'm fine.'' That was a lie. He was anything but fine. Still, no sense in upsetting Miss Winifred. It wasn't as if she could do anything about their situation.

He glanced up, caught her brushing away a tear.

''Did Luc tell you she has amnesia? That she can't remember anything?''

Miss Blessing nodded.

''Yes, he told me. But she's alive, Gray. And she's going to get better. You can thank the Lord for that.''

''Can I?'' Bitterness ate at his insides. Cody pressed against his knee and Gray lifted him up, held on to the little boy and tried to tamp down his anger. ''Can I also thank Him for allowing my wife to get her skull bashed in? Can I thank Him for taking my son's voice, for giving me months of unending misery when I didn't know if they were dead or alive? Can I really thank Him for all that, Miss Winifred?''

As soon as it was said, Gray wished he'd kept his mouth shut. But Winifred Blessing wasn't abashed by his anger. She didn't even flinch. Instead her quiet voice rolled over him like salve on a burn, soothing, easing away some of the sting as it cooled and refreshed.

''Yes, you can do all of that, son. You can rant and rave about the injustice of life till your cows come home.'' Her eyes sparkling, she lifted her head and dared him to debate her on this. ''Or you can get down on your knees and give thanks that God in His wonderful plan decided to give you and your family more time together, that He entrusted them to you for a little longer.''

''You don't understand,'' he muttered, lowering his voice as he became aware that Cody had homed in on the tension between them and didn't understand. ''I made God a promise that if He gave me a son and never let him go through the pain I experienced in my childhood, that I'd be the best possible father I could be.''

''And?''

She was staring at him as if he'd lost his marbles. Gray bristled, all his fears and worries massing together into one swell of raw irritation.

''What do you mean, and? I did the very best I could. I tried to be the kind of father I never had so that my son wouldn't go through what I did.''

''Yes?'' She looked like an inquisitive sparrow, head tilted to one side.

Gray stared at Marissa, the anger deflating like a pricked balloon. ''He didn't keep His side of the deal,'' he muttered.

''I see. So you made a deal with God.''

''Yes.''

"You set the terms, you decided how it would be fulfilled and now you've judged that God reneged. Is that about the gist of it?"

Put her way, it sounded a bit silly. But the meaning was there.

"Yes," he said, unable to stem his defiance.

"Uh-huh." Miss Blessing stared at him for a long time. Then she shook her head, lifted the white box from Cody's hands and held it out in front of his nose.

"You've got the wrong end of the stick in this relationship, Gray. And the sad thing is, you don't even know it. I'd like to stay here and hammer out who's who in your master of the universe game, but I've got to get to work. Furley is not as young as she used to be. In the meantime, chew on this."

She stuffed the box into his free hand, then turned and whirled through the door, charging off to cure the world. No doubt she'd unload the whole story on her assistant, Furley Bowes, and the two would confirm Miss Blessing's opinion that Gray McGonigle was an idiot.

Which was probably no less than he deserved.

Gray glanced down at Cody. "You okay?"

Cody's trusting eyes met his solemnly. He nodded. He glanced toward the door.

"I know. She was pretty ticked at me. But she doesn't understand."

Cody frowned, glanced at his mother, then at his father. Finally he took the box from Gray, lifted the lid and held it up so his father could look inside.

A giant heart-shaped cookie rested against a square of paper. Familiar red script across the cookie held his gaze.

Cody poked him, as if to say, "Well?"

Gray brushed his lips over his son's now-shiny hair, and sighed.

"Miss Winifred Blessing always has to have the last word, doesn't she?"

Cody grinned, reached out and pinched the V off the bottom of the heart. He popped it into his mouth, then lifted the cookie and held it toward his father. Gray nodded, read the message again.

"She sure knows where to hit a guy."

Cody giggled. The sound was like music to Gray's ears. Maybe Miss Win really did have a direct line to heaven for these messages. This one sure needed no explanation.

There is a God. You are not Him.

Chapter Four

"Okay, all your test results are in and everything seems fine. But just because I release you, it doesn't mean you're one hundred percent yet." Dr. Lucas Lawrence pretended to glare at Marissa. "I want you to take it easy, relax and enjoy being at home with Gray and Cody for a while. No lifting, no straining. No housework!"

She'd been here a week—long enough to heal most of her cuts and bruises. She was ready to leave the hospital with its bland food and weird hours. She was especially delighted by the thought that no one would wake her up to take a pill that put her to sleep.

But to go home? With two people she didn't know?

Marissa gulped, pretended to smile, watching as the doctor moved toward the door.

"No housework. Wow. That sounds pretty good."

"Consider it a reprieve. Knowing you and your penchant for organization, and remembering that Gray has been baching for almost six months, you should be grateful.'' He waved as he went out the door. ''See you in a few days, Marissa.''

A reprieve? More like throwing her to the wolves. The doubts multiplied a thousandfold. Marissa suddenly realized she had no idea what her home looked like, let alone how much cleaning it normally required.

And she had no wish to be there alone with Gray.

She knew no one would understand what she meant. They'd assume she was afraid of him. And she was. But it wasn't the ordinary kind of fear. Not the kind she felt when she woke from those awful dreams about the river. This was a different kind of fear, as if she might say or do the wrong thing and hurt him, erase that silvery glow in his eyes. Something drew her to him. It was as if she must somehow protect him, but she didn't understand that. Protect Gray from what, or whom—herself?

The past week had proven that the man who called himself her husband loved his son. The boy looked completely different. He had new clothes, for one thing. His hair had been cut, too. Not just hacked off, which was how it had looked the first time she'd seen him, but trimmed by an expert hand. But the most important thing was the way he giggled and laughed, ran and jumped, just like every other kid.

The only thing he didn't do was speak.

He'd often hug Gray's side, or lean his head against his leg when he was tired of waiting. Then his dad would scoop him up in his arms and the boy would snuggle down as if he belonged there.

Which he did.

It was Marissa who didn't seem to belong.

Oh, it was easy enough to bond with Cody. The boy

was adorable, and every time he brushed his chubby lips against her cheek, or hugged her, or snuggled beside her in the hospital bed, some inner spring wound a little tighter inside Marissa. She knew she was his mother, knew beyond a shadow of a doubt that she'd do anything to keep him from danger.

But when the nightmares came and ripped her fantasy world to shreds, when she had to face the fact that she might never remember his first steps, his first words, the first time he fell asleep in her arms—at those times she desperately wanted Gray McGonigle to be there for her, wanted his big strong arms around her, wanted to hear him say everything would be all right, just as he did with Cody.

Yet she pushed him away.

She had to.

To allow him to believe she felt something for him was to court disaster. Something had happened before her accident. Marissa knew it. She'd asked him, but Gray wouldn't tell her about that last day, wouldn't say much more than that they'd been happy. He was hiding something from her, and she longed to know what it was. Maybe then she'd be able to explain her turbulent emotions whenever he was near.

The truth was, she didn't know what she felt for Grayson McGonigle.

Gratitude? Indebtedness? Obligation? Curiosity?

All of the above.

His world must have been turned upside down when his family disappeared. But in the days since she'd awoken here, he hadn't once complained about his twice-daily trips into town to visit her, nor about her memory's lack of progress. He'd mentioned nothing about the extra help she understood he'd had to hire to help out with the chores while he took Cody to the city for tests. Even now, he didn't miss a beat about Luc's suggestion that they'd need home help because she was useless to him.

"I spoke to Miss Blessing about what Luc said. She knows a woman who moved back to town a while ago, after her daughter and grandson died. She has one other son, but he doesn't live with her. Anyway, apparently this Mrs. Biddle used to work for my father a long time ago, so she's used to the ranch, and she loves kids." Gray turned toward Marissa. "Does she sound all right to you?" he asked politely.

That he'd even bothered to ask was a mark of his consideration.

"She sounds fine." She edged toward the side of the bed, pushing back the pain that pinched her body. "Whatever you decide is fine."

She could see he didn't like her saying that. His eyes narrowed, his brows lowered. He looked frustrated.

"I'm sorry, Gray. It's not that I don't care. It's just that you should decide these things. After all, they have the most effect on you." She'd been trying to rectify whatever she'd said wrong, but was clearly only making matters worse. His jutting jaw was proof of that. She bit her lip, decided to stay silent.

"This affects you, too, Marissa. We can do whatever you want, but for now, I agree with Luc. You need rest and lots of it. A puff of air could whisk you away without even trying."

"I'm fine."

She glanced down, noticed his eyes staring at her

knobby knees poking out from the hem of her hospital gown and readjusted the thin cotton robe.

"Why didn't you put on your own robe and gown? I brought them days ago, but you still wear the hospital's. Did I bring the wrong things?" Gray stared down at the threadbare gown as if he couldn't understand her preference for such an ugly thing.

Well, why would he? He'd brought her an azure-blue velvet housecoat that begged to be worn, and a delicate white cotton nightie, with ribbon ties that matched the housecoat. They were beautiful and she'd have loved to snuggle into them. But they weren't hers. At least, they didn't *feel* like hers.

"I seem to have a lot of scrapes and cuts," she improvised. "I didn't want to stain anything, so I thought I'd save them until I was a bit more healed." She glanced behind him. "Where's Cody?"

"He's at school. I thought it was time to get him used to the routine. I've been taking him for an hour every morning. Today he's staying the full time."

"Oh." Which meant they'd be going to the ranch alone.

"You don't think it was a good idea?" He fiddled with his hat. "Maybe it is too much at once, but the doctors thought we should get his life as normal as possible, and..."

Now she had him second-guessing himself, something she doubted he'd ever done. Till now. On an impulse, Marissa laid a hand on his arm.

"Please, whatever you've decided is fine. I know you only want what's best for him."

"And you." He put his hand over hers where it rested against his muscled forearm. "I just want to make things better, Rissa. Inside, I know I can't. I know nothing will be the same again, but I have to do something. Otherwise I'll blow up.'' His fingers tightened, the lines around his eyes deepened. ''Every time I think of someone holding you against your will, of hitting you—''

She heard the torment in his voice, saw him strive for control. Then his arms were around her and he was holding her so tightly, she could barely breathe.

''Rissa, if you only knew how scared I've been.''

The words seemed dragged from him. It was the first time he'd really held her, though she'd expected it before now. There was no doubt in her mind that he cared about Cody but her, too? This much? Somehow that surprised her.

Something inside urged her to hold him, to brush that lock of recalcitrant hair off his forehead and kiss him there. But something else—some warning bell—reminded her that wanting to comfort him wouldn't be what he wanted from her. He was her husband, he'd expect—no! She pulled away.

''You don't have to be afraid. I'm all right. So is Cody. He'll talk to us when he's ready.'' She leaned back, putting a bigger distance between them. ''I guess I'd better get dressed.''

''I didn't know you'd be released today. I didn't bring you any clothes.'' He frowned at her, trying, she knew, to understand what made her so apprehensive she couldn't respond to him.

''I'll wear what I arrived in.'' She was pleased she'd thought of it so easily, until she saw him shake his head. ''Why not?''

''The police have your things. Evidence. They've

sent them away for analysis. Maybe they can find some clue about where you were held.'' His gaze moved down her body, focused on her feet. ''Seems funny you weren't wearing shoes. Your feet weren't cut or blistered, as they should have been if you were running barefoot.''

''Just another little mystery for you to unravel,'' she joked, drawing her toes under the hem of her gown.

He was discomfited for a moment, then his gaze landed on the rejected housecoat. ''I could go and buy something.''

''No, there's no need.'' She didn't want to be indebted to him further. Neither did she want to put off going to the ranch. It terrified her, but she had to do it or explain why not. It was better to arrive in the daytime, and it was already after lunch. If they waited any longer, it would be time to pick up Cody, and when she finally arrived home, Marissa didn't want the child watching her with those studious silver eyes that saw everything.

Home. How strange to think of it like that.

''I guess this is the only option, then.'' He held out the housecoat and gown.

''I guess you're right.'' She clambered awkwardly off the bed, took the items from him and headed for the bathroom. ''I'll be back in a minute.''

He nodded, but that curious lambent glow was back.

It wasn't the first time Marissa had been out of bed, nor the first time she'd seen a reflection of herself. But she still didn't feel she knew the stranger who stared back at her, so she tried to avoid looking that way.

Earlier her bandages had been removed. The nurse had helped Marissa wash her hair and now it hung loose and fluffy around her shoulders. Her scalp was tender, so she'd left the golden strands free.

The nightie had a soft fuzzy feel on the inside. Some kind of cotton sateen, she decided, sliding her hand over her midriff. The housecoat felt every bit as wonderful as it looked. Out of the shabby hospital gear, sheathed in this elegant finery, Marissa felt pretty. Graceful. Like someone else. Had she worn these things before?

"Rissa?"

A soft knock on the door alerted her to her husband's presence outside.

"Yes?" She froze, then told herself he had every right to walk inside if he wanted.

"Are you all right?"

She drew in a breath for courage, then pulled open the door.

"I'm fine. I was just trying to decide what to do about my feet."

"Good thing I happened along, then."

They both turned at the laughing voice. A man stood in the doorway. A tall man, sandy haired, with dancing brown eyes, looking for all the world as if he'd just stepped out of an ad for healthy outdoor living. He waited in the doorway, a gaily wrapped package in his hands. He wore jeans and a plaid shirt, but they were nothing like Gray's. There was no sign he'd ever done a day's work in either article. His snakeskin boots shone with a luster that proclaimed them new.

"Hi, sis."

Sis? This was her brother? Marissa scrutinized each feature, but found nothing familiar. Gradually she became aware of the tension sizzling across the room between the men. She glanced at Gray for an explanation.

"Marissa, this is my brother. Adam." The words were devoid of any emotion.

"Oh, come now, Grayson. Let's tell all the truth, shall we?" The debonair smile turned on her full force. "Everyone thinks I'm his half brother. The ne'er-do-well son who got gypped out of the ranch my father built with his bare hands." Malice glittered in Adam's eyes.

"I didn't gyp anyone." Gray grated the words out in a way that told her they'd gone over the same argument a hundred times before. "Harris left me the ranch, true. But you were well provided for, Adam. You could have bought your own place. If you'd wanted to." An implicit warning lay behind those quiet words.

"The point is, dear Marissa, that Grayson McGonigle, or whatever his real name is, shouldn't have received any portion of my father's inheritance because he is not my father's son. He's a liar and a cheat."

His real name? Marissa winced at the pure hate that seemed to thread through the angry accusations. She saw Gray's hands fist, saw his jaw clench and knew it was up to her to stop this from escalating, damaged memory notwithstanding.

"Look, I don't pretend to understand what you're talking about, Adam. I don't understand anything about my life. My head hurts, my body is stiff and sore and I feel like I'm in the middle of a tug-of-war. So if you don't mind, you two can carry on your feud, or whatever it is, later. Preferably when neither Cody nor I are present.''

''Aw, Marissa, I'm sorry.'' Adam's mobile face drooped with shame. ''I truly didn't mean to dredge that up again. I came to say I'm so sorry about the accident. How are you?''

''I'll be fine,'' she told him, praying she was telling the truth.

''I know that. You always had a knack for making things turn out good.'' He walked over, leaned down and brushed a kiss against her forehead. ''This is for you.''

She accepted the gift, surprised and pleased by his tender smile.

''Thank you, Adam. Though you didn't have to get me anything.''

''By the look of those toes, I did,'' he teased, peering down at her ankles and bare feet. ''Wherever you've been, you managed to get a bit of sun. At least on your feet.''

In unison she and Gray stared at her feet. Compared to the rest of her fair skin, her ankles and feet were tanned a light golden brown. Why was that?

She felt Gray's scrutiny. A wave of embarrassment washed over her at the intimate look. She busied herself opening the gift. A pair of slippers, fuzzy white ones with delicate little heels, lay against blue tissue paper.

She giggled at the silliness of them. Adam chuckled.

''I knew you'd like them.''

''Surely you didn't find these in Blessing?'' She laughed.

The silence unnerved her.

''What did I say?'' she whispered. Both men stared at her with an intensity that made her fidget. ''What's wrong?''

''You know where you live?'' Gray asked carefully. ''You remember the town?''

''No.'' She shook her head.

''Then how did you know that no place in town would carry these?''

Then she understood. Blessing. The town where they lived. She tried to figure out how she knew that, but nothing made sense.

''I don't know where it came from,'' she whispered, frustrated by the elusiveness of her mind. ''It just came out.''

''It's okay, honey.'' Gray squeezed her shoulder. ''It's great, really. It means things are starting to come back. The doctors all said not to force it, so let's not worry about that anymore. Why don't you try these on?'' He lifted a slipper from the box, carefully cradled her left foot and slipped the ridiculous footwear on it, then repeated the procedure with her other foot.

Marissa thrust out her legs and stared.

''I feel like Fifi La Ronge.''

''Who?'' Adam and Gray stared at her.

Marissa blushed. ''Never mind.'' She stood and practiced walking. Then she glanced around the room. ''Are we ready to go?''

Adam glanced at Gray. ''Cody at school?''

''Yes.'' Gray's stormy eyes met his brother's without flinching. ''He'll come home on the bus.''

''I could pick him up.''

''Don't bother. A neighbor's child will make sure he gets off at the right stop. I'll be there waiting.''

Adam shrugged, but Marissa thought she saw a glimmer of hurt in his dark brown eyes.

"Suit yourself. I was just trying to help."

"Really? You really want to help, Adam? Then why don't you pitch in at the ranch? I could use a lot of help there. Especially now." Gray's steady gaze remained pinned on his brother.

Adam's laugh held no amusement. Marissa saw his eyes harden, watched the snide tilt of his mouth transform her brother-in-law's charming face into a mask of petulance.

"My own father didn't think I had it in me to ranch, Gray. Why would you think any differently?"

"Maybe I see a side of you that Harris didn't." Gray glanced down at Marissa, but apparently decided to voice the rest of his opinion in spite of her presence.

"Harris loved you, Adam, and you know it. But he was afraid you'd gamble the ranch away just as you've done with the inheritance he left you." His voice dropped to a tone of quiet steel. "Anytime you want to come on board, you just let me know. I'm not trying to steal anything from you, but neither am I prepared to let you blow our father's lifework in some crapshoot. And until you can prove your allegations about my ancestry, I suggest you keep them to yourself. Marissa doesn't need the extra aggravation."

He drew her forward, toward the door. Adam stood in their path, but he silently stepped aside as they approached. Marissa paused, looked into his eyes and wondered at the hurt she saw there. Her heart ached for these two brothers so at war with each other.

"Thank you for my slippers, Adam," she murmured, reaching out to touch his arm. ''I like them very much.''

He caught her hand, squeezed it. His eyes opened wide when her sleeve fell back and he caught sight of the fading marks. His gaze flew to meet Gray's, asking a silent question.

''No, we don't know who did it yet,'' Gray murmured. He slipped an arm around Marissa's waist. ''At first I thought you might be to blame.''

Adam straightened, his anger visible, but Gray merely smiled that sad, painful twist of lips that mocked Adam's indignation.

''Don't worry. I soon realized that my own brother couldn't possibly want to hurt a woman who never did him any harm. Besides, Cody loves you, Adam. That's good enough for me.''

Marissa wanted to say something, anything to ease the anguish on the other man's face, but she couldn't think of a word. After several tense moments Gray heaved a sigh and solved the problem for her.

''Go ahead and pick up Cody, Adam. Only make sure you come straight home. Whoever did this is still at large. We'll see you there.'' Then Gray whisked her out of the room and down the hall before she could respond.

''What's the rush?'' she puffed, surprised at how quickly she became winded.

''No rush. Sorry.'' He adjusted his pace. ''They said they wanted to take you out in a wheelchair, but I'd like to avoid that, if we can. I've taken care of the paperwork.'' He helped her through a side door. Just beyond the curb sat a shiny black truck. ''Just in case someone is watching you, I'm not prepared to give them another opportunity to hone their abduction skills.''

He half lifted her inside, tucked her robe in around her and fastened her seat belt, then climbed into his own seat.

''Okay?'' he asked, his hand on the ignition.

''I guess.''

Truthfully, Marissa didn't know what else to say. It wasn't okay. Nothing was okay in this strange new world. But it wouldn't help to keep complaining about things. Somehow God would make sense out of the distortions in her world. She didn't know exactly how she knew that, but the solid comfort of the thought nestled down inside her heart and warmed her like a close friend. For the first time since she'd discovered her name, Marissa didn't feel alone. God was there. Watching. He would help her.

She sat back, prepared to take in every sight and sound that might give a clue about her home.

''Home'' took shape as a white rambling rancher-style house with a veranda just made to sit on and sip lemonade. It wrapped around the house as far as she could see, offering a fantastic view in every direction. The foothills had begun their autumnal color change, vibrant oranges and reds glowing in the late afternoon sun.

Marissa could only gaze in rapt admiration at the horses grazing in the pasture, at the herds of cattle dotting the golden hills and wonder at the beauty and serenity of this place that had been her home.

Why had she been afraid to come here? It was gorgeous. Yet even as she thought it, her eyes picked out a densely forested area far beyond the white fences. Prickles of fear made her skin crawl as she stared into the emerald-green of a coniferous forest. There were no bright tinges of red to lighten the ominous darkness, no yellow or orange streaks to break the shadowed duskiness she knew lay beyond that boundary.

"Marissa? Are you all right?" Gray stood beside her opened door, one hand upraised as if to touch her face. "I thought you'd gone into a trance. What's wrong?" He turned, surveyed the landscape, tried to find what held her attention.

"What's over there?" she asked, pointing.

He tilted his head back, peering across the land.

"Pastures. Grazing land. Hills. The creek. Why?"

"Does anyone ever go there?" she whispered. Her skin crawled with some nameless fear she couldn't quite repress.

"Sometimes I ride in to get a stray. It's pretty dense back there and very easy to get lost, but I leave it untouched because Harris, my father, wanted one piece of his property to remain wild. So did Dani's dad, on the ranch next door." He frowned at her. "Why are you asking?"

"I don't know." She shivered.

"Come on, it's cold out here. I should have brought your coat." He lifted her into his arms and carried her across the yard and up the stairs.

The door opened before he arrived. A tiny woman stood in the doorway, her silver hair wound into a complicated twist on top of her head.

"Come in, come in. It's getting cooler every day. I suspect winter will come early this year." She waited until Gray had set Marissa down, then held out one soft white hand. ''I'm Evelyn Biddle. Your husband and I talked earlier this morning. He said you'd want to interview me.''

''Interview?'' She looked to Gray for help. He didn't get a chance to respond.

''As housekeeper, dearie. Now come along, you just sit down in this big old chair in front of the fire. I saw the dust from the truck and knew you'd be along soon, so I made some tea. Would you like some?''

''Yes, please.'' Almost before she could blink, Marissa found herself tucked into the chair, an afghan covering her knees and a cup of sweetly scented tea in her hand.

''There we are. Now you just relax a bit. Winifred told me some of your story. It's a terrible thing. Just terrible.''

''Thank you.'' Winifred, that would be Winifred Blessing. If the kindly baker lady had sent this woman, Marissa was certain Mrs. Biddle would make a perfect housekeeper. There was something about Miss Blessing that inspired confidence no matter how long you'd known her.

''Whoever would do such a thing should be horsewhipped.''

''Um—''

Probably sensing her discomfort in talking about the past, Gray launched into a series of questions, which the older woman answered quite ably. Marissa sat and let them talk, content to listen.

''You must feel free to invite your own family to visit, Mrs. Biddle. Or take some time off. We can't keep you isolated out here all the time.''

The parchment skin drooped, the blue eyes faded, glossed over with tears.

"I don't have any family around here, dearie. My daughter was a widow. Army wife, you know. I was living with her and my grandson until they both died. Now I'm at a loose end. I have a son, but he won't be visiting me, I'm afraid. In fact, I don't see him often. He gets too upset. He's in a home now." She dabbed at her eyes. "I'd be glad to stay as long as you need my help. The fact is, you'd be doing me a favor. I just don't know what to do with myself anymore."

And she was probably short of money, if she'd been living with her daughter.

"I'm so sorry, Mrs. Biddle. I didn't know about your loss." Marissa was ashamed of herself. She'd been whining about her terrible life, which included a darling son and a husband who clearly cared for her. It was a life that would soon be filled with so many things. This poor woman had lost everything most dear to her.

"Don't you fret about it, honey. How could you know?" Mrs. Biddle shrugged. "A few months ago, after I'd spent a long time recovering from hip surgery, God seemed to tell me to come back to Blessing. I still have my little house, you see, even if it is rented. And at least one friend, Winifred Blessing. She suggested I stay with her, just until I got back on my feet. That didn't take long. I'm perfectly well now."

"I'm glad," Marissa said, and meant it.

"Winifred won't hear of me leaving. Says she likes the company. But when they found you, well, she was certain I could help. In a way, arriving out here today was a little like coming home.''

''Coming home?'' Marissa was tired. She struggled to make sense of the words. ''I don't understand.''

''Oh, of course you don't. It was long before you arrived.'' The old lady's eyes brightened. ''I used to live here, you see. Right here on this ranch. Young Adam and his mother lived here then.'' She glanced around the room, obviously reminiscing. ''I worked in this house for your husband's father. They were some of the happiest times I've ever known. Sometimes, when I think back, it seems like a dream. Harris was very good to me.''

''Then by all means, we'd like to have you come and work for us. When would you like to start? Though it looks like you've already begun.'' Marissa wasn't exactly sure why it seemed so important to try to restore some of the woman's joy, except that they were a perfect fit—Mrs. Biddle needed a home and a job, they needed a housekeeper.

Gray sat on the sofa, staring at her. He wore a bemused frown, but Marissa didn't think he was angry. Just a little surprised by her autocracy.

It would probably happen often, she decided. But after all, she was his wife—she was supposed to be in charge of things domestic. All right, then, she'd made her decision. Mrs. Biddle would stay and help her get used to being Mrs. Marissa McGonigle. If it was possible.

Adam and Cody burst through the door at that moment. Cody glanced at Mrs. Biddle, then walked carefully around her to climb into Gray's lap, grinning at Marissa. He held out a picture for his father to see.

"Very nice, son." Gray's head tilted down beside the boy's. "I think you'll be a painter, just like your mom."

"Hey, Biddie. It's good to see you again." Adam accepted the cup of tea from Mrs. Biddle, then held it aside to brush a kiss against her cheek. Clearly he already knew the woman and was comfortable with her. He perched on a stiff-backed chair in front of the picture window. "I've been meaning to ask about Randall ever since you moved in with Miss Blessing."

The voices faded away as Marissa stared past his shoulder to those dark shadowy bluffs in the distance. The sun would set soon. Then it would be dark out there, the shadows would dance among the trees, the wind would whisper secrets.

She shivered.

Something about that distant place made her nervous. But why? Surely if that's where their abductor had taken them, Gray would have found them long before five months had passed.

Unless he hadn't wanted anyone to find them.

They were in the house, with the boy. *His* boy.

He crept across the yard, careful to watch for the dog he knew would come running. But the dog was used to him by now and simply flopped his tail in greeting.

By crouching low, he could just peer through the side window. Good thing it was dark. No one could see him.

They were sitting around the kitchen table as if nothing was wrong, when his whole world was out of order. His eyes widened.

What was *she* doing there? Why had she come back?

To get his boy? Or to take him away, just as she'd taken the other one?

But she wouldn't keep Brett. Uh-uh. He shook his head. That was his boy, his special friend, and nobody was ever going to take him away again.

He had to think of a plan, a better one.

He stepped backward, froze when the planks creaked.

But no one heard. No one cared.

No one ever had cared about him—no one but the boy.

He had to get Brett back.

Chapter Five

Sleep should have come easily to Marissa that night.

Worn out trying to fit jagged pieces of memory together, learning of Adam and Gray's feud, combined with worrying that Gray might expect more of her than she was ready to give, she had sunk into a brooding chasm that she couldn't seem to pull herself out of.

But on the last issue, Marissa needn't have worried. Gray was kindness itself.

"I thought being in a familiar place might jog something, so you can sleep in our—in here," he murmured, showing her to the huge master suite at the head of the stairs. He flicked a switch and two wall sconces lit the interior, lending the furnishings a soft golden sheen echoed in the oak furniture.

"I moved my stuff into the spare room. Cody's across the hall." He waited for her to precede him into their room, waited for her reaction.

Marissa scanned the space, eyes wide as she took in the huge four-poster bed. She veered away from that, moved past the massive chest of drawers, barely glanced at the pretty makeup table. The huge floor-to-ceiling windows were uncovered, offering a gorgeous view of the valley below.

"I like this view," she whispered, surprising herself with the knowledge. "It's beautiful."

"It was your idea," Gray murmured. "We're facing east. The doors open, remember?" He clicked a mechanism and slid one glass pane wide.

She hadn't remembered. Marissa stepped outside into the coolness of the evening. Immediately she felt a flush of joy burst within as she stood on the circular balcony.

"This would be the perfect place to sip a cup of coffee in the morning," she whispered.

"You often did just that."

He stood behind her, not touching her, but near enough that Marissa knew he was there. His breath tickled her neck. She stepped a few inches away, tried to concentrate on the view.

The crispness of autumn was evident in the breeze that twirled a few leaves across the driveway. She looked beyond that to the pastures bound by white rails, then raised her eyes to the night sky. Thousands of diamond-bright stars dotted a sheath of midnight-black sky.

"Oh, look!" She held her breath as a band of white speared up from the mountains beyond, then twisted itself into a ripple of silver iridescence that undulated silently before them.

"Northern lights," she whispered. "How I've missed those northern lights. I haven't seen them for so long."

Sadness gripped her. "And the moon. Oh, look at the moon!"

A hand, warm and strong and utterly gentle, slipped over hers, cradling it as if to ease some of her sorrow. She turned, looked at him.

"I've missed a lot, haven't I?" she asked quietly. "And I don't even know it. It's like I've walked out of a tunnel."

His eyes, molten silver now, held hers until she felt the comfort he offered invade her soul.

"You're here, Marissa. That's all I care about." But the words didn't hide the tiny tic that flickered at one corner of his mouth, nor could it soften the harsh determination she could see in the rigid line of his jaw.

She didn't know what to say or how to answer. There were no words she could offer that would ease his pain or answer her questions. So she turned back to watch the night's display, and when his arms slipped around her waist and drew her back against his chest, she remained encircled by his strength, just for a moment, and tried to remember what it had been like to be loved by this man.

Eventually the lights wavered, the chill penetrated and Marissa shifted. There were no shortcuts. She couldn't be that person again, not until she remembered. She eased out of his embrace.

"You're cold. I shouldn't have kept you out here." He helped her through the doorway, then closed and locked the doors and drew the drapes. "Would you like to have a shower? Or a bath?"

She raised her head, stared at him.

"I could get Mrs. Biddle to help you." He rushed the words, his cheeks dotted red with color.

She looked away, shook her head.

"Thank you. But no, I'm too tired. I just want to sleep."

"Is your head aching again?" He led her to the bed, pressed her gently against the mattress edge until her knees bent and she was sitting. Then he slid off her slippers. "Luc sent some pills. I could—"

"No. No more pills." She jerked her foot away from him, knocked the slipper out of his hand. "No pills."

"Okay." He held up his hands. "I'm not going to force you. I just thought..."

She shook her head, fought to control her voice until she was certain her inner turmoil didn't show.

"No pills. I'm fine." She met his frown. "I will be fine, Gray."

He studied her for several moments. At last he nodded, lifted a corner of the bedding for her to slip beneath.

"If you need anything, just call. I'll hear you—it doesn't matter when." His hand rested against her cheek for a moment, as if he couldn't get used to the sensation. Then he leaned down and brushed his lips against hers in the briefest of touches. "Good night, Rissa. Sleep well."

"Thank you," she whispered, watching as he dimmed the wall lights until a faint glow lit the room.

He stood in the doorway watching, just for a moment, then slowly drew the door closed.

Marissa lay there for a long time. She tried to identify each bump and whisper in the big old house to see if she would remember something, but every sound, every noise seemed to tantalize her with some twisted meaning she couldn't unravel.

After a little while she climbed out of bed and drew the heavy silk draperies open. The moon was higher now, full and round, a huge orange ball that ducked in and out between the treetops. A few horses stood in one corner of the paddock, their heads tossing in the breeze.

Satisfied that nothing out there could harm her, she climbed back into bed and lay so that she could look through the windows, a prayer for courage whispering from her heart to God's.

Something rustled across her face, something soft and supple, with a delicate perfume she recognized. Marissa lifted her chin, allowed it to graze her neck.

Suddenly the softness was replaced by the rough harshness of strong fingers used to physical labor. A man's fingers. They grabbed at her, pressed her backward, out of the car, away from Cody.

"No," she screamed. "You can't take him. He's my son. I love him. Don't take him away. Please."

She reached out to grab Cody's shirt, anything, to keep him safe. The fingers were around her wrists, shackling her, rendering her struggles useless. Then she saw the car slip and slide off the road, over the edge, heard the rattling sound it made as it tumbled down the ravine, the crash when it finally came to rest.

But where was Cody?

Those fingers—she saw them squeezing tightly into Cody's shirt, half dragging him toward another car. They would not take him. Not without her. She followed, grabbed her son's arm.

"Leave him alone!"

Suddenly they were beside water, a big river that rushed past—whirling little eddies and brackish foam along the shore. The fingers tugged and pulled at Cody, pressing him toward the water.

"Be careful, my darling," she screamed, the warning burning in her brain as she watched in sick fear as he moved closer and closer to the dangerous rushing river. "Stay back. Wait for Mommy."

But Cody just grinned at her, then ran headlong into the rushing water. She tried to free herself, tried to go to him, but the hands, those terrible hands, would not free her, and the shiny brown head disappeared.

"Don't you see," she screamed. "He's drowning. Cody's drowning."

He was out of bed and across the hall at the first whimper from the room he'd shared with her for ten years. Marissa lay in the bed, blond head tossing back and forth as she struggled with an unseen attacker. Her hands lay palm up on either side of her head as if someone held her shackled.

"It's okay, Rissa. It's just a nightmare. Don't worry, honey. Cody's fine."

She fought him, tried to free herself, muttering something over and over.

Gray realized he wasn't helping and released her. He sat back, trying to talk her awake.

"Come on, baby. Cody's fine. You're having a nightmare, that's all. Cody's fine. Wake up, Marissa. It's just a dream."

"No. No, you're lying. You want to take Cody away from me."

"I would never do that, Marissa. I love him, too. Cody's asleep. He's in his very own bed. You don't want to wake him up now, do you? Shh. Let's not wake up Cody. He's so tired."

"No, he's not. Don't you see? Cody's in danger. He's drowning. Cody's drowning! Let go of him."

She lashed out at him, found his arm and dug in her nails. Gray winced, but kept talking. Gradually her grip lessened until her eyelids fluttered, then rose.

"It's okay, Rissa. I'm here. You're safe and Cody's safe. Everything is fine. You just had a nightmare, that's all." He brushed his hand over her mane of hair and repeated the words over and over until it seemed she absorbed what he was saying.

"Cody's okay?" Her face was shiny with tears, and as she sat up she dashed away the remainder. "Where is he? I want to see him."

"He's sleeping, sweetheart. He's worn right out from his first day at school."

She didn't believe him. He could see it in her eyes. And who could blame her? She'd spent the past five months protecting her child. Some day he'd tell her how much that meant to him.

"Come on, Rissa. I'll take you to Cody. You'll see that he's fine." He lifted the blankets, waited for her to climb out.

Her nightgown hiked up around her thighs as she wiggled herself out of bed. He caught his breath at the beauty of this woman who was his wife. Bruised and scratched, or dressed in the finest silk, she was perfect. He'd tell her that, too. Someday.

For now, Gray slid Adam's ridiculous slippers onto her feet, held out her housecoat and, when she slid her arms inside, turned her carefully to face him so he could tie the belt. His hands naturally slid over the narrow curve of her waist to her hips and he held them there, needing this touch more than he needed breath.

She stood silent before him, her eyes huge, fathomless as they stared into his. Fully awake.

"I'm sorry I woke you," she whispered.

He shook his head, touched her lips with his finger, traced their fullness.

"I'm not." He tried to smile. "I need to be here for you, Marissa. I need to be able to do at least that much." He swallowed the bitterness, concentrated on her. "Can you understand what I'm saying?"

She stared at him, then slowly nodded.

"You feel angry and helpless and you don't know what to expect. As soon as you make up your mind about something, you change it, wondering if that's the right thing, or the worst possible mistake you can make." She reached up, cupped his cheek in her palm. "I know exactly what you're not saying. You're afraid this will never end, that life will never be like it was before. Isn't that what's eating at you?"

He nodded, kissed her palm.

"How did you guess?"

"Because I go through those same feelings about a thousand times a day. At least you have the past to guide you." Her smile drooped, died. Her hand dropped away. "I have nothing," she whispered.

"You have me. You'll always have me, Rissa." He pulled her into his arms and just held her, trying to tell her without words that he would never let her go. "Somehow, together, we'll get through this."

After a few moments she pulled away.

"Us and God," she agreed. "Can I see Cody now? I can't remember which room—"

So the nightmare wasn't completely gone? He sighed, raked a hand through his hair.

"Sure. Come on." He grasped her small white hand in his and led her through the doorway, across the hall to the threshold of the room she'd spent ages decorating with huge murals and lifelike characters. He opened the door, then waited for her to step inside. For a moment sheer terror washed across her face and she seemed to freeze in place.

He slid his hands over her arms, brushing away the fear.

"It's okay, Marissa. Nothing's wrong. See the blankets moving up and down? That's him buried underneath. He always did huddle up like a caterpillar."

"Did he?" She stared down at the shape in the bedclothes. "I don't remember."

How could she not remember the baby she'd lavished her attention on? Gray felt the wave of frustration threaten and told himself to get a grip. What was *was.* They had to accept it and move on from there.

"C-could I see him? Please?" Marissa hugged her arms around her middle as if she were trying to protect herself.

What was wrong with her? Why was she acting like this? Gray frowned, shook his head.

"I don't want to wake him up, honey. He doesn't sleep as soundly as he used to."

Her eyes widened at his words, but her expression told him that nothing short of seeing her son sleeping in his own bed would do. Gray sighed, reached down and carefully freed the tousled head. Cody muttered something and wiggled in his sleep, twisting so his head was once more covered.

"He's all right, Marissa. You did a good job of caring for him. Cody's fine." He patted the boy's back, then straightened, did a double take.

Big fat tears coursed down Marissa's cheeks. Her gaze was riveted on the huddle of blankets as she stepped forward. One hand reached out, barely touched the blanket, then jerked away.

"I thought this time I'd lost him," she whispered. "I was so scared."

He turned her, his hands firm on her shoulders, and led her out of the room. Once the door was closed, he forced her to look at him.

"You didn't lose, Marissa. You won. You saved Cody, and you saved yourself."

She drew a big hiccuping breath, then nodded. "With God's help," she murmured.

"God?" The old animosity would not be silenced. "What did He do?"

"Everything." She looked toward the stairs. "Do you think we could make some hot chocolate? I don't want to go right to bed. Somehow I feel like hot chocolate would help. Call me crazy, but I want hot chocolate."

She wasn't crazy, merely acting true to form. Marissa had always loved hot chocolate, thick and rich, with whipped cream and cinnamon sprinkles or chocolate-bar shavings on top. He almost smiled at the memories of her lips rimmed with whipped cream, laughing at him.

"I guess there really are some things you never forget.'' He threaded her arm through his and led her down the stairs. ''Hot chocolate it is.''

He'd never mastered making it the way she did. Apparently she remembered that, as well. After watching him fiddle with things, Marissa took over as if she'd never left.

''You must always melt the sugar in the milk first, then add the chocolate,'' she told him seriously, discarding his burned effort. ''And never, ever stop stirring.''

He stood at the stove, dragging the spoon around and around, and watched her. She moved across the kitchen as if she'd never left, pulling out two of the big white mugs she favored, two long-handled spoons, the cream he'd never let himself run out of just in case she came home. Marissa wouldn't drink coffee without cream—real cream.

As he watched, Gray realized that in some ways her memory was perfectly intact. She knew exactly which cupboard held the hand whipper, how it came apart to go in the dishwasher. She even searched the cubbyhole where she used to stash her chocolate.

''There's only one left,'' she complained, frowning at him as she unwrapped the bar.

''You have it. I'm not big on that much chocolate this late at night anyhow.'' It wasn't true. He was big on anything she did. If she'd scrounged up a can of sardines and asked him to eat every one, he'd have done it, just for the pleasure of having her there, of having her ask him for something.

''I don't want it all. We'll share.'' She pulled open a drawer, lifted out her little grater and carefully reduced the bar to a pile of chocolate shavings. "You haven't let that burn, have you?"

He shook his head, amazed and delighted that at last she was back, here in her own home, where she belonged.

She took the spoon from him, turned off the element.

"Why don't you light a little fire? I think hot chocolate in front of the fire is nice."

So of course he lit a fire, built it too big, and then they had to sit back, away from the intense heat of it.

She handed him a mug.

"I hope it tastes all right," she murmured. "I haven't done this in a while." Her forehead creased. "At least, I don't think I have. That's the thing with this amnesia business. You're never quite sure."

"It's perfect."

"How do you know that? You haven't even tasted it." She wrinkled her nose at him, took a sip, then tilted her head to one side while she decided. "It's okay. I don't think that bar was very fresh. We'll have to go into town tomorrow—" She stopped, stared at him.

"You're remembering," he guessed.

"I don't know. Some things..." She peeked at him through the fringe of golden tendrils that clung to her forehead. "I had a nightmare tonight."

"I guessed." He forced himself to smile, knowing it wouldn't hide the grimness he felt. He'd never been good at that and Marissa had read him like a book.

"There was a man in the dream...." She frowned, closed her eyes, as if she might visualize him.

Gray only wanted her to forget the misery, but he

knew that was impossible. The perpetrator was still at large and he could return at any time. Anything she could remember, even a tiny detail, every snippet of information that could lead them to her abductor was a possible clue.

"Try to remember the man, Rissa. The police need any clue you can give. I know you were afraid of him, but try to recall something. Anything."

"Afraid of him?" She stared at him as if surprised, eventually nodded. "Yes, I suppose I must have been afraid. But not for me. For Cody."

He didn't understand what she meant. "This man, he wanted Cody?"

She nodded, the action vehement. "Yes, Cody."

"But he didn't want you?" It didn't make sense.

She frowned. Doubts clouded her sapphire eyes as she tried to unravel the threads. She lifted her head, stared into his eyes.

"I don't know," she whispered. "I can't remember. I'm sorry, but—I can't help you figure it out. I just can't remember."

The sadness on Marissa's face burned a path to his heart. Gray reached across, grasped her hand and squeezed.

"You're doing fine, sweetheart. You're here, you and Cody both. You survived. That's what's important."

She nodded, her fingers gripping his. Gray saw the ripple of concentration band her forehead, watched the shadows fill her eyes.

"He wore a hat." Her voice dropped to a whisper. "It matched his jacket. One of those army kind of jackets. You know?" She was lost in her own world.

All Gray could do was listen and hope she remembered something that would help them find this guy.

"A green jacket?"

"Well, kind of. Green and gray and brown. The colors kind of ran together. I tried and tried to look for him, but he was hard to see."

Camouflage. That's what she meant. The guy knew enough to wear clothes that concealed him in the woods.

"Cody loved looking at that jacket," she mused, rubbing her thumb against the tablecloth. "It had these sleeves you could zip off so that it made into a vest. And it had a ton of pockets."

She grinned suddenly and Gray's heart skipped a beat. She was so beautiful.

"He had everything in those pockets. A knife, a fishhook, a can opener."

His ears perked up. She hadn't told the sheriff that.

"What did he use the can opener for?' he asked, hoping his question wouldn't jar her out of her introspection.

"Opening cans." She sipped her drink, then shook her head. "I don't think I ever want to eat wieners and beans again. But Cody loved them."

So the fellow had had enough foresight to stock up on supplies.

"Where did you sleep, sweetheart?"

"In the cabin." She blinked at him, as if she expected him to know that. "It was okay. Cody and I had bunk beds."

The words slipped out easily, painting a clearer picture by the moment. He'd have to remember everything, pass it on to the police. The sheriff would probably race over to ask her more questions, though Luc had warned him that there was no schedule to these things. Marissa's brain would heal at its own rate.

''Why didn't you find us?''

The words shocked him out of his musings. Her hand shifted away from his, her blue eyes centered on him, dark, brimming with questions. Gray saw the doubts rush in and knew she was wondering, asking herself the same thing he'd asked a thousand times over in the past five months.

''That doctor, Luc?'' She waited for his nod. ''He said we'd been gone a long time. Did you give up?''

''No!'' He forced himself to calm down. ''Never, Marissa. I never gave up.''

''But then why—?''

''Why didn't we find you? I don't know.'' He blew a rush of pent-up breath from his lungs and drew in a cleansing breath to calm his anger. ''We found your car, the place where it went off the road. We searched the area for weeks. But there was no clue. Nothing to tell us where you'd gone.'' The gnawing emptiness of those interminable hours ate at his stomach like battery acid. ''We searched everywhere I could think of, but eventually we didn't know where else to look. The sheriff's men sent out bulletins, we put ads on television and radio, we had a missing persons team from the FBI assist us. But we couldn't find a thing.''

''You gave up.'' She was staring at her hands, knotting and unknotting her fingers as if she could discover an answer there.

''No, we didn't give up. I didn't give up, Marissa. Not ever.'' He tried to make her understand how frustrating the entire search had been. ''I finally hired a private investigator. I thought maybe there was something the police had missed, that he might have different ways of finding out stuff that would help. He came up empty, too.''

''Oh.'' She thought for a little while, sipping at her hot chocolate as she did. ''They said Cody was found near the church.''

He nodded, wincing at the memory.

''At the top of the ravine. You were found not too far from him, but nearer the bottom. Apparently someone hit you—'' He fought past the lump of outrage blocking his throat, forced himself to continue. ''The police think you must have rolled down after you hit your head. You were almost covered by the undergrowth when they found you.''

''Oh.'' She frowned, took another drink, then pushed out her tongue to collect the chocolate froth that clung to her lips. ''I don't remember.''

They sat together, sharing the silence but not really sharing anything because Marissa couldn't remember. Frustration chewed at him, but Gray tamped it down. It wasn't her fault. None of it was her fault.

''Can I ask you something?'' Her whisper-soft voice broke through his thoughts.

He looked up, found her clear blue eyes on him.

''We're married, Marissa. We don't have any secrets.'' Her tiny frown reminded him of that last day, the argument. She'd asked about that day before, but Gray couldn't go over it again, couldn't bring himself to remember the awful words.

''I happened to overhear you and Adam arguing again tonight. Why does he keep saying you've cheated him?''

Not again! *Go slowly. She doesn't remember the past. Explain.*

He sighed, raked a hand through his hair just to be doing something. When he had his emotions under control, he began.

"Adam believes my father owned a diamond, a very big diamond, worth a lot of money. When the estate was settled, he was to get half of the assets, but none of the land. Adam thinks I'm hiding the diamond, keeping it for myself."

"And you're not."

At least she sounded sure of that much about him. He ought to be grateful Marissa had that much trust left.

"I've never seen a diamond, never heard Harris—my father," he explained when her forehead wrinkled. "Harris never mentioned it. It's another mystery, just like that stupid horse."

"Horse?" She blinked, as if too much information had overloaded her brain. "What horse?"

She looked weary, her head wavering atop her slim neck, like a flower too heavy for the stalk. He cut the explanation as short as he could.

"Fancy Dancer. It was supposed to be a horse Dani's father traded for mine to pay for his ranch land. Dani is Luc's wife. You know, your doctor. They live next door. I rent their land, sort of. It's complicated."

She nodded.

"Yes, but one horse for land? That doesn't sound right, unless he was a racer or something."

"I know. It's crazy. I've gone over the books a hundred times and it still doesn't make sense. Why would my father give his valuable land for one horse, for which we have no records? The notation of land transfer is in his books, but it's never been paid off. It simply says Fancy Dancer, and the amount reads zero."

She closed her eyes, her forefinger rubbing a path above her golden eyebrows.

"Something," she whispered. "There's something..."

He sat silent, content to watch her. At this precise moment he couldn't have cared less about a diamond, the ranch or his father's disappearing horse. His wife was home, sitting in her kitchen. That was enough.

"Marissa?" She seemed in a trance, her pupils huge when she twisted to look at him. "You're tired. You need some rest."

"Yes." She nodded, rose, placed her mug and his in the sink and filled them with water, then clicked off the light above the counter.

"I'm ready."

He waited while she preceded him up the stairs, watched as she slid off her frivolous slippers and the housecoat he'd given her last Christmas. Then he walked to the bed and lifted the covers, waiting for her to climb in and wishing he could do the same.

She lay back, her hair splayed across the muted brown pillow. After several moments of staring, she turned on her side, smiled at him.

"You don't have to stay and watch me," she whispered. "I'll be fine."

"I want to." He pulled a chair near the bed and sank onto it, filling his senses with her.

"Okay." She yawned, tucked one hand under her cheek and let her golden lashes droop. "Good night."

"Good night." He touched her cheek with his fingertip, the silken skin transmitting a reaction straight to his heart.

She was asleep within moments, her chest moving up and down in a rhythmic pattern of sleep that was deep and even, dream free.

Gray sat there, keeping his lonely vigil, until memories of that last day intruded. Then it was too hard to stay, to look at her and remember.

He leaned over the edge of the bed and brushed his lips across hers, then straightened.

He almost made it to the door before the plea was torn from his heart.

"When you remember, Marissa," he murmured, one hand against the same door she'd slammed in his face that awful morning. "When you finally remember, please don't hate me."

Marissa slept on, ignorant of the pain squeezing his heart.

Gray turned and walked out of the room they'd once shared to return to the self-imposed exile that would never atone for the things he'd said.

Surely God was having the last laugh now.

Chapter Six

"It was a horrible dream." Marissa shuddered, then smiled into the concerned gaze Miss Winifred had fixed on her. "But it went away. Gray and I made some hot chocolate and talked in front of the fire. It was nice."

"I'm glad." Miss Winifred handed her a small square box. "I brought something for you and Cody. It's not much—just a couple of my love cookies."

"Love cookies?" Marissa took the box, a little confused by her meaning. "Well, thank you, Miss Blessing. But you shouldn't have. Mrs. Biddle told me you have a bakery to run. I'm sure driving out here wasn't part of your day plan."

"I'm glad to do it. I wanted to see how you're coming on. I know it's only been a day since you left the hospital, but you do look better, dear."

"I feel okay. Kind of dumb, maybe, but I'm learning. I just feel bad that Gray has to spend so much time on me. I know there are chores he needs to do before winter sets in, though I've no idea what they might be."

"Why would you?" Adam breezed into the room with no apology. "You had your own life to live. You certainly shouldn't have been wrangling cows."

"Now, Adam. You know Marissa never wrangled a cow in her life."

Marissa watched the unspoken interplay between the two. Miss Winifred seemed to be warning him about something, but she could tell from the belligerent look on Adam's face that he had no intention of heeding her.

"Why would she? She had her job and her painting and Cody. Not to mention this clunker of a house. It was enough to run anyone down."

"I have a job?" Marissa stared. "I'd somehow never thought of that."

"You worked part-time for a lawyer in town," Miss Winifred murmured. "It was while Cody was in preschool, just for a few hours a day."

"I overheard you saying your dream included a man." Adam's voice dropped. "Did you ever think that maybe your fear is because Gray was involved?"

"No!" The word burst out of her, but the moment she said it, Marissa knew it was true. Gray would not have hurt her or Cody. She might have forgotten alot, but not the fact that he loved them. Didn't he?

"You must hate him an awful lot," she whispered, staring at Adam. "Is that why you're saying this, because you want to drive me away so Gray would follow and you'd have the ranch to yourself?"

His face turned a bright red. He shuffled his feet against the worn carpet, shook his head.

"I don't hate him."

"Then why imply he was involved with my disappearance?" she demanded quietly. "It's mean and untrue, and not fair to the man who's offered you a place on this ranch if you'd only help him out. Is money so important to you that you'd slander him to get it?"

"You don't understand." His whole body sagged.

"No, I don't. You're brothers—"

"That's a lie! A pretense he carried on to influence my father so he'd leave him this land—*my land.*" His voice was loud, angry.

Marissa rose, walked to Adam, put her hand on his arm.

"Did you ever want to ranch, Adam? Until Gray was given the land, had you ever seriously considered spending the rest of your life here? Wasn't it just the means to an end—a way to get the money you needed to settle your debts?"

He glared at her, but Marissa continued.

"Gray loves this land, loves working it, watching it produce. He takes pride in the animals he raises, just like Harris did. Mightn't it be that you're jealous of that—jealous of the bond he and your father shared? Isn't that why you try so hard to blacken his name?"

"He's keeping the diamond."

"Adam, he doesn't know if or where any diamond is. He truly wants to help you, but he can't hand over the ranch and watch you cut it up in small chunks to sell to the highest bidder. That would betray the trust Harris put in him, and you and I both know Gray could never do that."

He was silent for a long time. Then his eyes widened.

"I thought you'd lost your memory." His face tightened. "Or were you just pretending, like him?"

Marissa spared a moment to wonder how she'd known to say those words, where her assurance came from. But did it really matter? She couldn't let these two men, brothers, be torn apart any longer. She had to do whatever she could to make both men see the other's side.

"I don't remember anything more than I did, Adam. I only know what I've been told and what I feel here." She laid a hand over her heart. "You're angry and hurt by Harris's decision to include Gray in his inheritance. I understand that. Your father had an affair with another woman while married to your mother. He betrayed her in the most hurtful way a man can. And you felt your mother's pain."

"She left him because of it," he muttered. "Neither of them wanted a divorce and I got shunted back and forth. All because of Gray McGonigle and his mother."

Marissa gulped down her tears.

"Oh, Adam. Gray is as innocent in this as you. He didn't do anything wrong, but he paid dearly because his mother wouldn't tell Harris about him. Harris lost all those years when he could have known his sons. Everybody lost, Adam. Isn't it time it ended?"

How did she know all this? Where were the words coming from? Though Marissa could answer neither of those two questions, something compelled her to continue.

"Maybe you feel a little uncertain of your father's

love, Adam, or that it was in some way diminished by Gray's presence.'' She shook her head. ''That isn't true. Love isn't meted out in tiny parcels. Given a chance, it takes root and grows to encompass. Because Harris had two sons doesn't mean he loved one any less.''

''You don't understand.'' Adam turned away, but Marissa would not release his arm.

''I think you've known me for a while, haven't you, Adam?''

He nodded.

''Then let me ask you something. If Gray and I—'' She felt the burn of embarrassment flood her face, glanced at Miss Blessing watching them. The subject was intimate, private, not something she could even think about yet. But this was important—she couldn't afford to hold back. Besides, it was the best analogy she could come up with at the moment.

''If Gray and I had another child, do you think I would love Cody any less?''

''No.'' He shook his head, his grin wide. ''You're a born mother. You'd love the next one as much as you love that kid.''

She nodded.

''It was the same with Harris. He didn't push you away. I think you did that to him. Don't do it to Gray, too. Life is too short—family and love are too hard to come by.''

He stood there staring down at her for a long time. He reached out one hand to touch the mark on her forehead.

''You've got a lot of nerve, Marissa.''

"Is that normal for me?" she asked, peering through her lashes.

He threw back his head and laughed, his eyes dancing with mirth.

"I'd say it's perfectly normal for the Marissa McGonigle I knew. Thanks." He bent, brushed her cheek with his lips, then turned and left as quickly as he'd come.

Marissa slumped a little, found her way to an armchair and sank into it.

"Are you all right, dear?"

She glanced up, found Miss Blessing's gaze on her.

"I think so. Just a little tired, I guess." She leaned her head back against the soft chenille and closed her eyes.

"Well, why not? It takes strength and energy to fight for those you love."

Marissa blinked. Love? Did she love Gray? She didn't know that whatever feelings she had could be categorized as love. She had few doubts about his love for Cody. Everything he'd done pointed to his care for the boy—and for her. But what were her own feelings?

"Don't fuss about it, dear. When the time is right, you'll know your heart. Until then, why not take a nap?" Miss Blessing picked up a fuzzy pink afghan and draped it over her, lifted her feet onto an ottoman and set the bakery box aside. "Later, if you're hungry, you can munch on those. Perhaps you'll find the words encouraging. I'll tell Mrs. Biddle to let you sleep."

She moved to the doorway, paused there for a moment.

"You know, when I came out here, I was a bit worried about this family. Now I realize God has everything firmly under control.'' She smiled. ''Good-bye, Marissa. Take care.''

''Bye.'' She yawned, watching Miss Blessing close the study door behind her. How had she become so tired? Did it matter?

Marissa decided not and let her eyelids drop, but then remembered the box. Curiosity would not be stifled, so she reached out and lifted it onto her lap. She opened the lid and peered inside.

Two white heart-shaped cookies lay protected by parchment paper. One had a smiley face on it and Cody's name. The other had tiny red words piped across its surface.

A candle loses nothing by lighting another candle.

She frowned. Meaning? She could almost hear the older woman's soft voice admonishing her to keep trying to mend the fences separating the two brothers. Or perhaps she meant that one memory would lead to another.

Marissa closed her eyes and searched for other explanations, but she decided to do it with her eyes closed. It was just too hard to keep them open.

Gray sat on the uncomfortable stool and stared into his coffee cup as the gossip around him swirled. Coffee row. He'd rather be riding the hills on the hottest day in August wearing long underwear than sitting here drinking this swill and listening to the old boys gossip. But he had to put in time until Cody's specialist could see him. Another ten minutes or so, and he'd go back. Then, once he knew the truth, he could break it to Marissa.

''Owes a pile of money. Really went wild after his

pa died. I hear the crunch is on now they're asking for it back, and those good old boys are the kind you don't argue with."

He froze, forced himself to pay attention. They were talking about Adam. He knew that. The sharks his brother had borrowed from must have blabbed to someone.

Ever since Harris's death, the McGonigle brothers had been the talk of the town, with only brief respites from the gossips when Nicole Darling had come to town and set about straightening out Joshua. Luc Lawrence's appearance after Joshua's accident had given the tongues something else to wag about, especially when Dermot DeWitt had passed away and his daughter, Dani, couldn't be found. The plight of her ranch and her romance with the Blessing township's newest doctor had fueled yet more scuttlebutt, but the scandalmongers always returned to the subject of him and Adam.

"You hear what the kid's into them for?"

Gray closed his eyes as the amount was given. So much? And Adam hadn't said, hadn't even hinted that he was so badly indebted.

Or had he?

With so much on his plate, Gray admitted to himself that he might have missed something. But what was he to do? Adam didn't want to help on the ranch, and Gray couldn't, no, wouldn't just turn over Harris's life's work.

"Hey, Gray. I didn't know it was you sitting over here. How are you? And how's Marissa?" Phillip Thornbush's too white teeth glinted in the late afternoon sun.

"She's fine, thanks. Feeling better every day."

"Good, good." Phillip accepted his change from the waitress, but made no move to leave. "Say, I was wondering, Gray. She say anything about when she might be coming back to work?" The town's lawyer shuffled in a very un-Phillip-like way.

"She hasn't said, Phillip. In fact, I don't think she's even remembered that she was working for you. Why? Marcy taking a holiday?" Gray knew very well that Marcy Williams had used her holidays in August to go back east to see her mother. And Phillip knew he knew.

"No. Nothing like that." He picked up his foam cup of coffee. "Walk out with me, will you?"

What was this about?

Gray slapped some change on the counter and followed him out the door, conscious of all the interested eyes that accompanied him.

"Truth is, I don't want to rush Marissa at all. I'd like to see her recover fully before she even thinks about coming back." Phillip kept his eyes on the window across the street.

"Then...?" The purpose of this chat stymied Gray, but he figured it was worth biding his time to find out what was behind it.

"The truth is, Marissa was going through some old files before she...disappeared. I only remembered the other day because I had to dig back through some of Dad's notes on a client's father." Phillip's father, Ephraim Thornbush, had built the law practice that Phillip now ran. Ephraim still came in, but less and less frequently. Golf had become his new passion.

"Thing is, the file is gone. I was kind of hoping she might have taken it home."

Gray shook his head.

"I haven't seen it. And I would have, in the past five months. It wasn't in her car when they found it, either. That would have been a clue." He spat the words out bitterly, but his mind was churning the information, trying to find a reason Marissa would have been rifling through Ephraim's old files. She hadn't come from Blessing, wouldn't know any of the old gent's former clients. Unless it was someone still alive.

"Okay." Phillip nodded. "Well, that's what I thought, but I had to check it out. I don't like those documents to be on the loose."

"Marissa never brought work home. And I'm sure she wouldn't steal it, Phillip." He visually dared the man to say otherwise.

"No, of course not! Don't worry. It will probably turn up, misfiled or something." Obviously realizing he was now accusing Marissa of botching her job, he shook his head. "Just forget about it. I'll get Marcy to go through things again."

"If she remembers anything about it, I'll have her phone you." Gray watched him walk away, his leather jacket flapping in the breeze.

"Do that, Gray. And tell her hi from Marcy and me."

All the way to the hospital, Gray mulled over the unusual encounter. He sat through the consultation, heard the same words he'd heard a thousand times before.

Posttraumatic stress, they'd decided. Be patient, let him talk when he's ready. Keep Cody feeling secure and life would soon be back to normal. Nothing had changed.

But something about Phillip's comments nagged at Gray, forcing him to think back. Marissa had been acting oddly that last morning—with a sort of suppressed excitement. Cody had asked to take his favorite toy to preschool, and for once Marissa had encouraged it when she usually insisted he leave the little glass figurine at home.

Had Marissa learned something from a file that made her a threat to someone? Or had she found out something about his relationship to Harris, something that would have made her doubt him?

But surely, that afternoon when she'd phoned before she'd left to pick up Cody, she would have said something? All she'd talked about was Fancy Dancer. He'd told her to forget it, and she'd insisted that if such a horse existed there should be records. She'd even brought Adam into it. He remembered what had followed and thrust the conversation from his mind.

The past was over, finished. It was the future they needed to concentrate on.

As he drove back to the ranch, Gray wondered if he'd ever again experience something as wonderful as normal. He would have liked to ask for some heavenly assurance, but that was hard when you weren't talking to God.

When Marissa woke from her nap, Mrs. Biddle had some delicious soup ready. Gray had gone out to check on something with their newest colt, so the two ladies sat in the kitchen and chatted for a while. Then Marissa changed into a pair of jeans and a thick sweater. Ratty old sneakers waited at the back door and, assuming they were hers, she pulled them on, eager to explore before walking down the road to meet Cody.

Wild daisies still bloomed in profusion in a small garden to the side of the house. She deadheaded a few with the scissors she found hanging on a nearby wall, clipped others for a vase for the table and gave them to Mrs. Biddle. The dog came racing up and she rubbed and patted her as if they were old friends, grateful for the immediate acceptance of an animal who clearly knew her.

The walk to meet Cody's bus, while not overly long, was tiring, especially climbing the steep incline. Just beyond that was a small hollow that met the main road. Here she found a mailbox mounted on a post with "McGonigle" neatly printed on one side. She was pretty sure that when the little flag pointed upright, there was mail inside.

Though she had no idea if this was her job or not, Marissa opened the door and lifted out the few letters and a newspaper that lay inside. There were some bills, a couple of cards offering discounts at a local food chain and two flyers. Under these she found a small yellow envelope with her name printed on it in childish letters. "Marissa."

Cody, she decided, smiling at the crooked letters of red crayon. Perhaps he'd stuck it there that morning when he'd met the bus with Gray. Perhaps it was a secret he wanted to tell her but couldn't say, so he'd chosen to share it this way, though it saddened her that he hadn't written "Mommy."

She tore the flap open and slid out the single sheet of lined paper, torn from a notebook.

"He's mine. You can't have him. I'm going to get him back. Keep away."

Her suddenly nerveless fingers loosened as the fear rose like a specter from the past. Her entire body went cold, though the air hadn't changed. She watched stupidly as the wind grabbed the paper and tore it away, carrying it to the pastures beyond.

She should have chased it, Marissa's mind argued. But she ignored that voice because the bus came trundling over the hill. *Please God, let Cody be on it. Don't let him be gone.*

Then she saw the red fuzzy sweater, the clear gray stare, and almost wilted with relief. He was safe. She knelt on the grass and gathered him into her arms, hugging him as tightly as she dared. The bus door closed and the vehicle departed, but Marissa had eyes only for her son.

"I love you, Cody. Do you know that?" In that second she realized the truth of her feelings. Her memory might be impaired, she might have some things to relearn, but this one thing stood stark and clear in her mind.

She would do whatever it took to keep this precious child safe.

Cody blinked, then nodded, obviously confused by her sudden embrace. His stomach rumbled. Marissa held her breath as his giggle tumbled out. He opened his mouth and she was certain he'd say something. But he didn't. Instead, he patted his tummy.

"Hungry, huh?" She pretended nothing was wrong and grabbed his hand. "Miss Winifred was here this morning. She brought you a cookie. And Daddy got some chocolate milk for you after he dropped you at kindergarten. Will that help?''

Cody nodded. Once they were within five hundred feet of the house, she let go of his hand and watched him race ahead, the dog bounding beside him. In her fingers she held the yellow envelope, though everything in her yearned to let it go and get rid of this feeling that someone was watching.

Gray came riding up before she got to the house. He pulled his stallion to a stop beside her, smiled at her with those serious gray eyes.

''You look cold, Marissa. Maybe you should go inside.'' His gaze moved to her hands. ''Anything interesting in the mail?''

''Someone left me a note,'' she whispered. ''But it blew away. I just have the envelope left.''

In a flash he'd dismounted. His hands clung to her shoulders, holding her a few inches away as he searched her face.

''What did it say?'' he demanded, his face drained of all color.

''I don't remember exactly. Something like, 'He's mine. You can't have him. I'll get him back.' Something like that.'' She stared at him, the fear a tangible taste in her mouth. ''Who is doing this? And why? What did I do wrong?''

''Nothing. I don't know why this is happening.'' He rested his chin on her head for a moment, then stepped back. ''Come on, we've got to call the sheriff's department. At least we've got the envelope to show them.''

The rest of the afternoon passed in a weary round

of questions that had no answers. Marissa hated watching the lines return to the edges of Gray's mouth, hated seeing his shoulders slump as he admitted he had no clue who the perpetrator might be.

Supper that night was a quiet meal. Cody continued his self-imposed silence, though his eyes showed his worry as his glance roved from his mother to his father. Marissa helped him prepare for bed, then sat on the edge, waiting for him to choose a story. *Black Beauty.*

His favorite.

Marissa gulped. How could she know which story her son loved and not remember giving birth to him? What was wrong with her?

"Cody?"

He lay on his back, his glossy brown head resting on the pillows that were covered in cowboys. He looked at her, his big eyes wide with a question.

"I need to talk to you about the person who took us away from here. Okay?"

His eyes darkened, his lips tightened. But after a moment he nodded.

"Daddy told you I can't remember anything about then, didn't he?"

Again the nod.

"So I wouldn't remember if that person came to our house." Maybe this wasn't such a good idea. Maybe she would frighten Cody unnecessarily. But what other choice did she have? She couldn't let them take her son again. She had to do something.

"I'm not saying that person is going to come here," she murmured, hoping that would reassure him. "Daddy's here and he would protect you. It's just that if they showed up somewhere, at your school maybe, would you do something for me?''

He frowned.

''Would you not go anywhere until you tell me first? Please? Because I'd be so worried about you. I know you don't want to talk about that time, Cody. I know it scares you. But as long as Daddy and I are here, we won't let anything bad happen to you. We'll make sure you're safe. But we want you to help, too. Because that's what families do. They help each other. And people shouldn't try to break up families. Do you understand?''

He studied her for several moments, then sat up and threw his arms around her neck, hugging her tight.

''I love you, Cody. I love you very much.'' She held him as closely as she could, breathed in the soft citrus scent of his freshly shampooed hair and whispered a prayer for God's protection on all of them.

But later, when the nightmare returned, she didn't wait for Gray to comfort her. She tiptoed across the hall and into her son's room, just to make sure he was all right.

She watched his sweetly snoring body lifting the covers up and down, waited for some reassurance to return. When it didn't, she hurried back to her own room, grabbed a quilt and made herself a bed beside his.

No one was going to take Cody away from his daddy again.

No one.

Chapter Seven

Gray was glad Marissa had gone into town with Mrs. Biddle for her checkup. That way he wouldn't have to explain.

He sat nursing his coffee, wondering if it was wrong to suspect your own brother of kidnapping. After all, Adam's motive had been made clear two days earlier when Gray had overheard that conversation in the coffee shop. Money was a powerful motivator.

But it didn't make sense. Adam hadn't disappeared for the past five months. Nor was it believable that Adam would have hurt Cody. Still, he'd seen his brother riding the fertile valley pasture early this morning. And now Gray was missing two of his pedigreed bulls, animals that had been grazing in the valley just yesterday.

And then there was the problem of that cut in Marissa's saddle.

Gray had pulled both hers and Cody's down last night, intending to polish them before he suggested a ride and a picnic on Saturday. Now he wondered just how wise that would be. He'd assumed his family would be safe here, on his land.

Maybe he was wrong.

About everything.

The phone rang.

"Gray? This is Phillip Thornbush."

"Hi." His mouth curled automatically, but he kept his voice level. "What can I do for you?"

"I just wanted to tell you—remember the matter we discussed the day before yesterday?"

He made it sound as if they'd shared some furtive assignation.

"Yes. The missing file. Did you find it?" Gray tossed back the rest of his coffee before realizing it had gone cold.

"Yes. Yes, we did. I don't know how Marcy missed it, but it's here." Phillip clicked his tongue in an exact imitation of his father.

"Good." Gray almost said goodbye, but then had another thought. "Do you mind if I ask whose file it was?"

"I'm not really—why do you want to know?"

"Just curious." Gray shrugged. "I guess I was hoping it might give me a clue as to why they disappeared. It's pretty frustrating not to have any reason for your family going missing for almost half a year, you know."

"I imagine it is." Something like sympathy was transmitted across the phone line. "I don't know how this could possibly help you, but on the off chance that it might, I don't see any harm in explaining. It was Dermot DeWitt's file. You might remember that his estate was the last my father handled before he got it into his head to retire to the golf links.''

Gray thought back. Dermot had died before Christmas. He remembered, because his death was sudden and his daughter couldn't be found. Dani had left the college where she'd been studying. Later she'd turned up on the Double D and been aghast at the extent of the problems that had worried her father. She'd been halfway to solving her problems before she learned that Dermot owed Harris money for land he'd bought but only paid for with Fancy Dancer.

Gray had known about the debt since Harris's death, of course. But he'd kept silent because he hadn't known what deal the two old men had worked out and because Dani had enough problems to deal with. But Dani had insisted on paying him the full amount. Then she'd offered Adam the Double D and said the rent would go toward the interest she owed as long as he didn't alter the river land her father had loved. Since he needed the extra grazing land, Gray had taken over the DeWitt spread until Adam could get back on his feet and run the place.

Only, Adam never had. He'd left town.

And now he was back.

''Gray? Are you there?''

''Yeah, Phillip. Just thinking. Thanks for telling me.''

''Does it help?''

''I don't know.'' He hung up the phone, went back out to the tack room and began mending the tears. There was no point in calling the police. He had no idea when the cut had been made, how long it had been there. He only knew it had to be fixed.

He'd almost finished when Adam sauntered in.

"Do you know you have some bulls loose?"

"What?" Gray wheeled around, frowned at Adam. "Loose where?"

"On the road in. I almost hit one of them. They seem to enjoy the grass on the other side of the fence. Want a hand getting them back in the pasture?"

It was the first move Adam had made toward him and Gray wasn't about to turn it away, regardless of what had gone between them before. Besides, he'd already fallen far behind in his chores. Another hand would help.

"That'd be great. That black one has a hair trigger, so watch yourself."

"Yeah, I remember." Adam rubbed his leg, no doubt recalling a previous altercation with the angry beast. "Why don't you get rid of him? He's way past his prime."

Gray shrugged, remembered.

"Marissa wanted to keep him. Said he'd done his part for the ranch, and now it was up to us to see to his retirement." He tossed his saddle onto his stallion, spared a moment to watch Adam do the same.

"Worried I've forgotten how to saddle a horse, Gray?" Adam's laughing eyes held a glint of anger.

"Not really. Just remembering something." He turned away, tightened the cinch, checked his reins. "I guess it wouldn't matter if I got rid of him now. She wouldn't even notice."

"She will remember, Gray. One of these days she'll get it all back."

He studied his brother, wondered where he got his assurance from.

"Don't tell me you think her memory loss is permanent?" Adam's voice echoed the disbelief on his face.

"I don't know what to think anymore. I've gone over it a thousand times, trying to figure it out. Nothing makes sense." He decided to tell the truth. "Today I found this." He turned Marissa's saddle over, pointed to the slash.

Adam whistled, his finger tracing the deep cut to the leather made by a very sharp knife. "This is dangerous."

"I know. But how long has it been there? That's the thing. I haven't looked at it in months. It could have happened anytime."

Adam shook his head.

"I was out here when she was in the hospital. Thought I'd make sure things were ready if she wanted to go for a ride." He looked away from Gray's scrutiny, obviously embarrassed. "You know how she liked to go to the river, to sit on that big rock and watch the trout jump. I just wanted to make sure that when she remembered, everything would be ready." He looked up, his eyes deadly serious. "There was no cut then."

"So it's happened since she returned."

"Meaning?"

"Meaning someone followed her here. Meaning they're not about to give up." He related the incident about Marissa's letter. "It was directed at her, but the letter suggests it's Cody they want."

"Why? He's just a kid. It doesn't make sense."

"None of it does." Gray vaulted into his saddle.

"Come on, let's corral those bulls. I was certain they were grazing in the valley."

"They were. I saw them this morning."

"What were you doing out there?" He walked his horse out of the barn, waited for Adam to catch up.

"You'll think I'm nuts."

"It won't be the first time." Reading the guilt on his face, Gray grinned. "Racing Duke again?" he asked, lifting one eyebrow. "Dani will box your ears if anything happens to her horse. You know that?"

"She's explained it to me once or twice." Adam's serious look worried Gray. "And no, I wasn't racing. Not really. Just riding. Thinking." He clicked his teeth at the big sorrel, urged him forward. "I saw something."

Gray froze.

"Something? What?"

"I don't know, not exactly. At first I thought it was a person, sitting on that hump—you know the one."

"Parker's Hump." Gray nodded. Everyone knew about the hillock that overlooked the ranch. "Who was it?"

"Nobody. When I got there, all I could see was a big bunch of long grass wavering in the wind. I'm no tracker, but there was a flat spot—as if someone had been there. I kept riding, just in case I found a trespasser. But I didn't see anything else."

They worked together in harmony, corralling the bulls, then moved them into a pasture much farther from the house.

"Hey, Gray?" Adam paused, loosening his rope just a little. "Did it occur to you that Cody might have come down here, walking from the bus?"

Gray jerked his head around to stare at his brother, all energy draining from his body. Sanity returned slowly.

"No! Marissa always meets the bus."

"Then..."

Neither one wanted to say what the other was thinking. But Gray could see his thoughts reflected on Adam's face—the loose bulls might have charged Marissa.

"This is getting nasty," was all his brother would say.

When the fence was safely closed, the two of them headed back to the house. It was Adam who made the coffee, poured him a mug and added a dollop of cream.

"I don't take cream," he argued, staring at the milky concoction.

"Since when? You've been buying it for six months. How was I supposed to know you got it to dump down the drain?" Adam shrugged. "Just drink it, okay? Then we'd better come up with some kind of a plan."

A plan? What kind of a plan could protect his wife from this nebulous phantom of fear? Who knew where it would strike next?

Still, an offer of help from Adam was not to be turned away. Gray gulped down the coffee, felt it move through him, warming him. Then he remembered.

"Adam, did Marissa say anything to you about something she was hunting for in Phillip's office? Before she...went away?"

"Went away"—a stupid euphemism for the reality

of his wife's abduction. He tamped down the anger in order to concentrate.

"Phillip's?" Adam shook his head, face perplexed. "I don't think so, but it was a while ago and a lot's happened since. It's kind of hard to remember. Why?"

"I don't know. Just something he said that bothers me, I guess." Gray looked up, found Adam's eyes fixed on him. "He asked me if she'd brought home a file. Dermot DeWitt's file."

Adam's eyes widened but he said nothing, merely leaned forward, intent on hearing the rest of the story.

"Apparently he couldn't find it and Marissa was looking at it or in it right before she disappeared. He assumed, since he couldn't find it, that she'd taken it home."

"Well, she did have a soft spot for the old coot." Adam scratched his head. "But he died...must be almost a year ago. Why would she be poking through his file?"

Gray shrugged. He had no answers. Only another ton of questions. But now was not the time.

"Adam—" He stopped, wondered if he should be trusting someone who obviously hated him. But what other choice was there? "I need to ask your help," he blurted out.

"My help?" Adam frowned. "For what? And why? We haven't exactly trusted each other so far."

"Then maybe it's time we did." Gray was well aware he couldn't do it all. He had to take a chance with someone. Why not Adam? "I've been thinking about whoever did these things—the letter, the saddle, the animals."

"The bulls could have been an accident."

Gray raised one eyebrow.

''Okay, so there was no broken fence. But I just can't believe that someone from around here, someone we know, would do that to Marissa and Cody.''

''What makes you think it was someone we know?'' Gray watched him puzzle it through. ''I started out thinking that, too,'' he muttered, ''but it doesn't have to be. It could be a total stranger. Given the right motive—'' He left the rest up to his brother's imagination.

''Which would be what? None of it makes any sense.'' Adam swatted at a fly, then rose to pour them both another cup. ''Especially you asking me for help. Maybe you'd better explain. You need help around here—is that what you're trying to do? Con me into working the ranch for you?''

''Not exactly.'' Marissa would skin him alive if she found out what he was doing, but Gray could think of no other way to protect her and Cody. ''I was hoping maybe you'd hang around, keep an eye on my wife and son while I'm working.''

Adam stared at him.

''Whoever is doing this has walked onto our land at least twice, probably way more than that. They've left a threat for Marissa and they've damaged her saddle.'' He clenched his fists at his impotence. ''They're moving about freely, doing whatever they want, and I can't stop it. If they make a move for Cody—'' He left it hanging, hoping Adam would see how serious this was.

''So you want me to—what? Stop by every morning? Marissa will see through that in a minute.'' Adam shook his head. ''Way too obvious.''

''I wasn't thinking of you stopping by. I was thinking you might move in.''

He waited, bracing himself for the verbal assault that would accuse him again.

But Adam didn't say anything, merely sat there, studying him.

''You're really that worried?'' he asked quietly.

Gray nodded.

''Why don't you call the police, ask them to send someone?''

''Too obvious. They'd stand out like a sore thumb. Besides, what would I tell them—that I was afraid?'' He shook his head. ''They were useless before.''

His brother said nothing.

''Marissa would offer to have you here if she thought you had nowhere to go. You've been shacked up at the Double D, haven't you? Must be getting a little cool at night. And then you have to get your own meals. Mrs. Biddle makes a pretty mean roast.'' He heard the desperation in his own voice and wondered if Adam noticed.

''Gray, your wife will notice if I suddenly start accompanying her everywhere. She knows I wasn't around here much before—''

''She doesn't, though. Don't you see, she can't remember what it was like before. I've thought about this long and hard. This is the schedule I've come up with.'' He laid it out, each step of the day, how they'd choreograph watching over his two loved ones.

''You don't have to be obvious. She can't drive—not yet anyway, so you can take her into town when she needs to go. I don't imagine it will be long before she finds her paints. She's always settled in with them once the leaves turned color.''

He wasn't going to go for it. Gray could see it in his eyes. Desperation gripped him.

''All this babble you've spread around—you know it's not true, Adam. Harris had the paternity tests done. They were positive. He even admitted he'd had an affair with my mother all those years ago, that they fought and she left him. Why keep pretending there's nothing between us?''

''Because there isn't.'' Adam sucked in a lungful of air, then whooshed it out. ''You're his son by blood. I was adopted.''

''Don't be stupid!'' Irritation rose as Gray assembled all his arguments. But then he glanced at Adam, saw that he believed it. ''Why are you saying this?''

''Because it's true. Marissa knew. I told her ages ago.''

Marissa knew—and she'd kept it a secret from him? What else had she withheld?

''But—but…'' He stumbled for the right words. ''Harris was married to your mother. You were born here, on the ranch. You are his son, Adam. Why do you doubt that?''

''Look at me, Gray. I don't look anything like him. Everyone could see the resemblance between you two, but no one ever recognized any resemblance between him and me.''

''You're being foolish, Adam. Of course you don't look exactly like Gray. You had different mothers. But that doesn't mean you weren't Harris's son.''

Gray whirled around, saw Marissa standing in the doorway.

''How—how long have you been there?'' he demanded, fingers gripping the arms of his chair.

''Long enough.'' She dropped her packages on the table, lifted her jacket off her shoulders, hung it on a peg nearby. ''I don't need a protector, Gray. But Adam is welcome to stay here. I promise I won't let him out of my sight.''

Gray swallowed his groan. This was *not* his day.

A few moments later Mrs. Biddle also entered, a shopping bag hanging from each hand.

''Looks like you cleaned out the shops.'' Adam tried to get a peek inside Mrs. Biddle's bag. ''Is that for supper?'' he asked when she lifted out a chocolate layer cake.

''Don't ask me! Marissa made me buy it. Why, I don't know. Always do my own baking. Did it for your father, and I thought I'd be doing it here. Don't hold much with store-bought.'' She smacked the plastic container on the counter and shoved it to the very back as if afraid it might contaminate her.

''Miss Winifred gave it to me. You know I couldn't refuse, Mrs. Biddle. She's a friend and she's been very kind to me. To us.''

Gray watched Marissa coax the other woman to relent.

''You know she's a great baker. And you've been running yourself ragged trying to keep up with everything around here. Why shouldn't I get a cake from the Blessing Bakery, if it makes things easier for you? Besides, Adam's going to be here. He loves cakes. You'll never be able to keep up.'' She bent over and kissed the blustering woman's red-tinged cheek. ''Now stop fussing.''

"Huh! Next thing you'll be buying me one of her love cookies, I suppose."

"Maybe." Marissa winked at Gray, her smile wide and full. "If I think you need it. Is there anything special you'd like her to write on it?"

He caught his breath at that smile, remembered how she'd loved to tease.

"You know very well that she only writes messages that she feels are from above." Mrs. Biddle's eyebrows floated upward. "I certainly wouldn't be the one telling her those!"

"Uh, it's almost time for Cody's bus. I'll go, if you don't mind." Adam lifted one eyebrow at Gray.

"No, you won't. I'll meet the laddie myself. I baked some cookies for him, fresh this morning, and I want a chance to offer some before he stuffs his face with Winifred Blessing's cake." Mrs. Biddle buttoned up her thick wool sweater and marched out the door.

Gray glanced at Marissa, wondering what had prompted this from a woman who'd barely spoken since she'd arrived. Marissa's eyes glittered, her mouth twitched until finally she burst into delighted laughter.

"I've got to paint her." She giggled as she unpacked the rest of the supplies. "I'm going to call it *Righteous Indignation.*"

"So you've remembered. I wondered how long you'd be able to keep away from your daubs of color." Adam glanced over one shoulder, grinned. "Righteous indignation suits her."

But Marissa didn't answer him. She was too busy staring at Gray.

"I paint," she murmured. "Pictures."

He nodded.

"Good ones, too." He jerked a thumb toward the door. "What happened with her? I thought she and Miss Blessing were good friends."

"They were. Are." Looking slightly bemused, Marissa slid the milk and cream into the fridge, took the cans Gray held and lined them up on the cupboard shelves so their labels were facing out, each one half an inch from the edge.

She'd always been like that, he realized. Precise, organized, everything in its place. He wondered if the place she'd been staying in was as well managed.

"So what brought on this 'righteous indignation'?" Adam asked.

"Winifred suggested Gray needed coddling." She avoided his eyes, concentrated on Adam. "She claims he's lost weight and is too skinny, though Mrs. Biddle insists he is certainly eating enough."

"They were arguing over me?" A slow heat rose to burn his cheeks, got hotter when they both stared at him. "I'm fine. I'm always fine." He hated all this attention, so he turned to his wife. "You're the one who had the doctor's appointment. What did he say?"

She didn't answer him for several moments. Gray grew concerned, but he was afraid to ask too much with his brother present. Fortunately, Adam's perceptive abilities were still working. He pushed back his chair.

"I, uh, want to show Cody something when he arrives," he mumbled. "Excuse me."

Gray waited only as long as it took Adam to close the back door. Then he reached out, grasped her elbow and turned her to face him.

"What did Luc say?" he demanded, the fear bulging inside his heart.

"That I'm not sleeping enough. Okay?" She rifled through her purse, pulled out the small package and shoved it toward him. "He told me to take those. More pills! As if I haven't swallowed enough."

He took them, glanced at the words. A sedative—mild, but still more than she'd ever needed before.

"I don't want to be doped up! I want my mind to be clear, focused. I want to think, to remember. I *do not* want to depend on drugs to get me through the night."

"You're not going to depend on them. They're just an aid, to help you through the rough spots." He lifted one hand, brushed it over her dancing curls. Since she didn't protest, he reached out, drew her into his arms, pressed her head against his shoulder. "Marissa, Luc's trying to help. You know this can't go on. You get up every night to check on Cody. You sleep on the floor, too. That can't be very restful."

She jerked her head back to stare at him.

"Yes, I know all about your little midnight trips. Did you think I wouldn't hear you? That I wouldn't notice?" He allowed a smile to surface, though it hurt to realize she didn't understand how much he cared.

"Doesn't sound like you've been getting much sleep, either." She sighed, then nestled back against his chest, as she had so often in the past. "Maybe *you* should take the pills."

"They wouldn't help. I don't sleep very well without you," he murmured into the delicate shell of her ear. "I miss you."

In an instant he could feel the tension ripple through

her muscles, and he chewed himself out for his stupidity. As if their…separation was her fault.

"I'll be fine, Rissa. I'm not recovering. You are. And if Luc says you need to take a pill to help you rest, then you take it. Okay?" He tipped up her chin so he could look into her eyes. "It's not as if someone's going to sneak in and steal Cody while you're out cold."

From the way her pupils dilated, he knew he'd hit a nerve. He was shocked. Six months ago his wife had been afraid of nothing.

"Is that why you're getting up, Marissa, sleeping by his bed? Because you think his abductor is coming back to get him?"

For a long time she remained silent, staring at him. Then her head moved, just the slightest nod.

"Yes."

That whisper-soft admission did strange things to his heart, squeezing it so tight he could hardly breathe. He could feel the fear tremors ripple through her. She was afraid here—in her own home! Anger rose like molten lava, eating deep to his soul.

Why didn't God do something? Why keep torturing her?

"I'll take the pills, Gray. Don't worry."

At once he swallowed his anger—enough that she couldn't see, at least.

"Sweetheart, you don't have to be afraid. Nobody's going to take Cody. I'll make sure of that. I don't want you to make yourself sick over it. I want you to get healthy and strong."

"You want the old Marissa back." Her tone was

flat, unemotional. ''But I don't know if I can be her anymore. So much has changed.''

''You be yourself and that will be just fine with me.'' Gray hoped he was speaking the truth, but if he had to guarantee it, he wasn't sure he could. He wanted what he'd had six months ago—he wanted his past life back. He wanted whomever was hounding them to be gone from their lives. Permanently.

He wanted to be free of the worry, the wondering if he'd missed something, failed to notice some clue that would explain. Most of all he wanted to be free of the never-ending nagging in his gut that reminded him he was powerless to stop the same thing from occurring tomorrow, or any morning after that.

''It's something I've got to come to grips with,'' she whispered. ''Fear isn't from God. 'Perfect love casts out fear.' I've just got to trust that He knows what's happening and why, that He is in control.''

She stood in the circle of his arms and repeated the words over and over, impressing them on his brain in the process. But even after Cody bounded through the door and Mrs. Biddle began the procedures for dinner, he couldn't dislodge those words.

That night, while the harvest moon shimmied its way over the horizon and shone down a warm orange hue over the land he loved, Gray sat beside his wife and watched her sleep. Every twenty minutes or so, he rose, checked on Cody, made sure the doors were locked.

Marissa could trust God. He had to make sure for himself.

The big farmhouse perched on the hill like some kind of ghostly picture from the past. He'd spent a lot of time on a tire swing just like that when he was a kid, straining to get it higher.

Now he crept around the edges, avoiding the rosebushes that didn't used to grow so close to the veranda. Some toys were lying by the bottom step and he picked them up.

"Brett's toys. I'll keep them for him." He slipped them inside his pockets.

At the top of the steps, farther along the wide porch, there were two willow chairs. One of them held something. He moved closer, tiptoeing over the boards to avoid the creaks.

Whatever was on the chair was hidden by a white sheet. A surprise! He loved surprises—good surprises. He hadn't had a good surprise in a very long time. Maybe it was a gift. From Brett.

He stepped too heavily against the house and one of the boards made an awful racket. It almost scared him away. But he had to see under that sheet.

Fingers shaking, he reached out, snatched away the covering and stared.

It *was* a present. For him. The best present he'd ever received. Maybe *she* was sorry now. Maybe she wouldn't try to run away again.

He picked it up, carefully tucked the sheet around it and moved off the veranda, away from the house and into the night with his prize, his mouth wide with glee.

He'd put this in their special place—their very special place.

And every night, before he went to bed, he'd look at it, until he got Brett back.

Because Brett belonged with him.

Chapter Eight

Marissa stood in the tack room, her body motionless as her fingers grazed the soft velvety feel of Gray's suede jacket.

The texture was so familiar. Why was that?

"Is something the matter?"

She whirled around, stared at Adam.

"I've startled you. I'm sorry."

"It's...okay." She pressed her fingers against the nap once more, then let go, watching as the sleeve sprang back to hang against the coat. "I was just thinking."

"I can see that." He frowned, moved closer. "What's wrong, Marissa?"

"Why should anything be wrong?" She didn't want to tell him, or anyone, about the nebulous feelings she was having. But some things just wouldn't be silenced. Except at night—after she took the little white pill.

"Never mind. It's probably none of my business anyway." He turned to leave.

"Wait!" She bit her lip, watched him freeze, then turn, his face confused. "There's something familiar about this jacket, Adam. Do you know why?"

"Gray's hunting jacket?" He shook his head. "Like what? Like you wore it or something? It's not new, if that's what you mean."

"Did I ever wear it?"

"Not that I know of." He kept watching her, his eyes assessing every detail, as if she were some kind of specimen.

"Hello, dears. No one was at the house, so I figured you'd be down here." Miss Winifred bustled through the door, fought to close it behind her. "My word, that's an awful wind!"

"Hi, Miss Blessing. How are you?" Marissa forced a smile to her lips. *Don't act like a weirdo around her, too,* she ordered her mixed-up brain.

"I'm fine, dear. It's you I was concerned about. You didn't come to church on Sunday." The baker's blue eyes darkened, pinning her with their intensity.

"No, I didn't." Marissa flushed. "I—I couldn't face the thought of everyone staring at me, and not knowing who they were. I was hoping—" She let the words die away, knowing it did no good to say them.

"You were hoping to remember something before you had to face them all again, is that it?"

"Yes. I guess so." She shrugged, pretended a smile.

"In God's time, dear. All in God's own time."

"But how do I know when that is?" The frustration of her blank mind ate at her much as a dog gnawed a bone. "What am I supposed to do in the meantime? Sit twiddling my thumbs? Cody's at school, Gray's busy. Even Adam—'' She turned to look at him, realized he'd slipped away while she'd been speaking.

''Everyone's been wonderful to me, but they have stuff to do and I don't want them to fuss. I want to be normal.''

''You are normal. But you're finding the hours are long, hmm?'' Miss Winifred nodded her understanding. ''Have you thought about returning to your part-time job?''

''Marissa doesn't have to work. She needs to stay home, relax and get better.'' Gray stood in the doorway, his eyes darkening to steel.

For the first time since she'd met the baker lady, Marissa saw anger flash through Winifred Blessing's faded blue eyes.

''You mean you want to keep her here so you can control her movements and prevent her from disappearing again? Isn't that what you really mean, Grayson?'' Miss Winifred marched up to him, stopped only inches away. ''You can't box her in, make the ranch her jail. Life must go on. People change, things happen and we try to make the best of it. It's just the way it is.''

''She's in danger if she leaves here.'' He sidestepped Miss Winifred, wrapped his arm around Marissa's waist.

Immediately reassurance flooded over her, and Marissa knew she didn't want to go back to whatever work she'd done. She wasn't sure why she thought that—she just knew it was so.

''What protection do you think you can offer that God can't better, Gray? Marissa has never been out of His sight, not even once. He knows every hair on her head, He sees her heart. And yours.'' She moved closer, and her voice dropped. ''When are you going to start trusting Him, son?''

''I can't.''

The stark pain embedded in those words shocked Marissa. Somehow she hadn't realized how much he was hurting. Something to do with his focus on her, perhaps, instead of letting her help him.

''Can you tell me why?''

''Because—'' He shook his head. ''Never mind.''

''Because maybe He'll take them away again, permanently? Because maybe He's punishing you? Is that what you think?'' Miss Winifred was relentless in her pursuit.

''Yes.''

Gray's fingers tightened painfully tight against her side, but Marissa couldn't, wouldn't move an inch. Instead she threaded her own arm around his middle, pressing herself closer.

As far as she knew, she'd been kidnapped along with Cody, taken away and held somewhere that was not her home for over five months. She had cuts and bruises, marks, scratches—but those were already fading. She didn't know why it had happened or who had done it. In fact, she remembered very little beyond the scattered fragments of her dreams.

Yet one thing stayed certain in some corner of her brain, sustained her through all the blank spaces. God would help her get through this.

But Gray—he'd been left behind, abandoned without any explanations or reasons. As the days and weeks had passed with no answers, his mind had conjured up things far worse than anything she dreamed about. In that instant she understood what to do next, how to help him as he'd tried to help her—it was her job to support him now and she didn't intend to fail. At this moment she had to show him that no matter what the past had been, the future was theirs to build—together.

She whispered a prayer for guidance, then let the words tumble out without thought. Maybe not remembering wasn't so bad after all. That way you weren't afraid of what you might say.

"Gray, do you remember when Cody was learning to walk and he fell, bit through his bottom lip?" She felt a fractional easing in his muscles, knew he was listening. "I have no doubt in my mind that God could have made that table move, could have turned Cody away, or eased his fall, but that didn't happen. Does that mean God *wanted* a sweet innocent baby to get two stitches?" She shook her head. "Of course not. God didn't cause that. Cody did, by trying to breach the natural laws that say if you hit wood with your chin, it will hurt. Laws that He gave for our protection."

She blinked, peeked up at him through her lashes and wondered if she was making sense.

"But God *could* have stopped it. How could He just sit there and watch a child in pain?"

His whispered question broke her heart. But Marissa knew she had to be the strong one now. She had to help him see that he was blaming the wrong person.

"Because He is God. Because He won't go back on his decision to give us free will to make our own decisions, even though He could save us so much pain and heartache, just as we could have saved Cody that bump if we'd forever carried him on our hip. But because of that one instance, Cody learned to negotiate carefully around the furniture.'' She threaded her fingers into his, squeezed them.

''There could be a hundred reasons that we don't know about, and never will, but the fact is I've lost my memory and Cody isn't speaking. Okay. Now we have to deal with that reality. We have to get on with living.''

He frowned and his lips moved, but she cut him off.

''I know your childhood was awful and that you were always afraid Cody would go through the same thing, but he hasn't, Gray. He didn't. That's because God has kept His hand on that little boy, not because He was waiting in the wings to punish you. That's not God. He's not that small.''

''But Cody doesn't speak.'' The words signaled how deep his hurt went. ''Not even to me.'' *Not even to his father* was what he meant.

She nodded.

''I know. Not yet. But he will. The doctors say he will, in time. We just have to wait until he's ready. And have faith.''

Marissa took a deep breath, then said the one thing she knew he wouldn't want to hear.

''But, Gray, what if He did decide that it was time for Cody to go to heaven? Do you think you could stop it? Could you stop God?''

His eyes darkened until the silvery-gray turned almost black.

''No! He can't!''

The groan ripped from him and Marissa knew she needed help. She turned to Miss Blessing, trying to appeal to her without saying anything. Winifred seemed to understand, for she stepped forward, clapped a hand on Gray's arm and spoke.

"But He can. Therein lies the crux of the problem, son. You don't get to decide. You're not God. You put your faith in Him, and then you lean on Him to handle whatever He deems best. You can't have it both ways, Gray. You can't tell him He's Lord, and then be your own boss. Faith is an all-or-nothing proposition."

"It's asking too much."

"It's asking you to take Him at His word, to trust."

He sighed, his shoulders slumping with the weight of this decision.

Whatever he would have said at that moment was stalled as the door flew open and Cody raced inside. He glanced wildly about the room, then raced toward Marissa, wrapping his arms around her legs and hanging on so tightly she thought she might have toppled over if it hadn't been for Gray's strength.

"Cody?" Bit by bit she loosened his arms, then hunkered down so she could see into his eyes, those silvery beams so like Gray's. "What's the matter, honey?"

His entire body trembled. He glanced from her to Gray, his lips working. But no sound emerged.

"He was like that when I met the bus. I could hardly keep up with him." Adam smiled at his nephew. "He runs like the wind."

"Cody?" Gray's icy voice forestalled any other comment. Cody stared at his granite face, then took one step backward. Gray reached out to grab his arm.

"This is important, son. Did you see the bad man again? The one who took you and Mommy?"

It was painfully obvious that Cody wanted to speak and equally obvious that he was afraid of something, or someone. His eyes searched Gray's, then flew back to Marissa's, his lips parted, then clamped together.

"Is that what happened, honey? You can tell us, you know. We just want to stop him from taking us away again. He can't hurt you. You're here with us."

Myriad emotions flickered across Cody's face, but at long last he shook his head, then turned and shuffled back to the doorway.

"Come on, Cody. Let's go sample some of Mrs. Biddle's gooseberry tarts. Did I ever tell you the story of the gooseberry tart?" Keeping her voice even and calm, Miss Winifred tucked his hand into hers and led him back toward the house.

"He saw something. I'm sure he did."

"So what are you going to do? Beat it out of him?" Adam leaned against the doorpost, a frown marring his handsome face. "You've got to get hold of yourself, Gray. If he did see the guy, for some reason he's not telling. You keep this up and he won't. You scared him pretty badly."

Gray's head jerked in an angry nod.

"Good. Because I'm scared! There's a madman loose, in case you hadn't noticed. I want him put away." The enmity between the two men filled the air with tension.

"But why wouldn't Cody tell us if he was back, Adam? He knows we're only trying to protect him." Marissa rubbed her eyes with her knuckles. "Oh, I wish I could remember something."

"You will. When you're ready. Just don't push it."

Gray heaved a sigh, pulled her hands away. "Adam's right."

"Never thought I'd hear that." Adam chuckled at Gray's red cheeks.

"Well, you're hearing it now. I blew it, and I've probably made things worse. I need to apologize to Cody. I don't want him to be afraid to come to me. Not ever."

"You can do that while we have coffee. I'd say it must be about time for a break. Besides, we've got two bakers over there. I want to see which one wins this round." Adam's wicked grin brought a smile even to Gray's face as he held the door open.

As they trooped back to the house, Marissa was conscious of the coolness of the wind as it whistled down from mountains wearing caps of fresh snow. A wiggle of worry climbed up her spine as she stared at the dark, lowering trees in the valley beyond. There was something about those trees—

"It's beginning to rain. We'd better run." Gray grabbed her hand and half led, half pulled her onward.

But as they mounted the steps of the veranda, Marissa suddenly remembered.

"Wait! I've got to get something." She raced around to the other side, praying the droplets hadn't blown away the sheet, washed away her pale watercolors. But the painting of Cody was not sitting on the chair where she'd left it. In fact, it was nowhere in sight.

She stepped forward, leaned over the balustrade and stared at the surrounding countryside as the wind whipped her face, tore at her hair.

Could it have blown away? But where?

''Marissa, it's going to pour. Look at those clouds. You'll get soaked. Come on.'' Gray stood behind her, tried to urge her inside. ''What are you looking at?''

But she barely heard him. Inside her mind, that voice issued words she'd heard before.

You'll never get him back. He's mine. Forever.

Holding one hand to shield her eyes, she stared across the land to the forest of trees that had bothered her since that first day. What was it that sent a wash of dread over her whenever she glanced at them? She pushed away all thought and allowed her mind to take over. Almost she could make out a face. Almost.

''Marissa, come on!''

Whatever she thought she'd seen blurred in the sheets of rain that now poured from the leaden sky. Disappointed that her brain refused to yield even one clue to the past, Marissa turned reluctantly and walked inside the house.

Miss Blessing turned to her while the others teased Cody about his sneakers with the flashing lights.

''What's wrong, dear?'' she asked, her voice modulated so no one else could hear.

''Nothing really. I suppose I'm just moping.'' Marissa motioned to the door. ''For a moment I almost thought I remembered something. But then it was gone. It's so frustrating.''

''Ah.'' Winifred nodded. ''I wondered why—'' She stopped in the midst of her sentence and walked to the counter, where she retrieved one of the little white Blessing Bakery boxes with the familiar red script, ''Blessing Bakery—made with love.''

''Perhaps this will be of some help, Marissa. I

wasn't sure I'd heard the words correctly until just now.''

Heard the words? Marissa puzzled for a moment, then remembered Gray saying something about the baker's penchant for claiming the advice she gave so freely came from God.

She opened the box, peered inside.

Defeat isn't bitter, if you don't swallow it.

''Do you understand what it means, dear?''

Amazingly, Marissa did. She knew it as clearly as she knew anything these days.

''Yes, I do. Thank you very much, Miss Blessing.'' She reached out and hugged the older woman.

She'd chided Gray about his fear, but wasn't it time she faced her own? Those dark hills with their thick woods had bothered her long enough. It was time to face them down. Maybe then her brain would release the information she so desperately needed.

Saturday morning dawned with the crisp clarity that only an autumn day provides. The air was sharp, invigorating, the colors purely vivid. Was it the angle of the sun that made the greens seem more verdant, the reds, golds and oranges just that much more intense?

Marissa touched the bag behind her saddle to reassure herself that she'd packed her paints and her sketchbook. The undulating acres of land framed by granite peaks feather-dusted against the saturated blue sky were too good to miss.

''Are you regretting your decision?'' Gray cantered alongside her, his forehead pleated in a tiny frown. ''We don't have to go there, you know. We can leave it for another time.''

"No." She stared past her horse's head to the gloomy forest and shook her head. "We'll picnic, as we planned. I'll sketch a bit, then I want to go on. Whatever's back there, I need to see it."

They took their time, neither rushing nor dawdling. Marissa tried to gauge her response as they got closer to the woods, but then wondered if her nervousness came from riding again, from watching Cody atop his pony, or from something else, something in her past.

Mrs. Biddle's lunch was exactly right—thin slices of roast chicken on freshly baked bread with a touch of mayonnaise, celery and carrot sticks, crunchy apples and ginger snaps for dessert. Gray and Marissa shared a thermos of coffee while Cody sipped lemonade.

While Gray snoozed and Cody climbed a tree, Marissa found herself too tense to paint. Sensing her frustration, Gray suggested they continue the journey.

"My dad and Dermot DeWitt made a deal to keep this area as natural as possible, so we don't let the animals back here. The trail is pretty rough."

His side-glance told her he didn't think she was strong enough. But Marissa knew better. She had to do this. It was time.

"I'm fine." She nudged the horse on, bending her head to avoid the low-hanging boughs of massive fir and spruce.

They weren't far into their foray when Cody turned to look at her, his eyes huge with unasked questions. Perhaps she'd been foolish not to leave him behind, but somehow the two of them with Gray made this a family thing. Strength in numbers—wasn't that what people said?

"It's okay, Cody. We're just going for a ride on Daddy's land. Just us three. There's nothing to worry about." She smiled reassurance until he nodded, turned around and continued to follow Gray.

The deeper they penetrated the forest, the tighter her neck muscles pinched. There was little sunlight here, even though the ground was a carpet of yellow and orange. Wavering boughs thick with needles held out the light in a canopy above.

They were moving down a sharp incline now and Marissa's horse stumbled. She leaned forward to pat his neck and saw herself picking up dead branches from the forest floor. The driest were best for starting fires. Then you didn't use too many matches. *He* didn't like fires that smoked and took a long time to light, so she was extra careful about which wood she chose.

Just as suddenly as it had come, the vision was gone and Marissa was astride her horse, fingers clenched around the reins. What had she remembered? But though she tried to re-create the scene, it wouldn't come.

She became aware that they'd stopped. Cody trotted his little pony over beside her, frowned as he stared into her eyes. Gray noticed.

"Marissa?"

"I'm...fine. Let's keep going." She tried to keep the elation she felt from showing. It wasn't much, but it was something. At last, a memory. Maybe there would be more if she kept going.

The trees are so thick, they don't allow much light through. Maybe that's why I can remember bits. It's like my dream.

But as eagerly as she waited for the next revelation,

nothing more transpired in the hour it took them to reach Dani's cabin.

"It's quite lovely here. I didn't realize we'd left your land." Marissa dismounted, relieved to be out of the saddle for even a few moments as they took in the view.

"We're not far from it, but this is Double D land. Dani specifically requested she keep the title on her dad's river property. I don't mind. I've never had much time to come back here. Our side is a lot rougher than this piece. You can't really ride into it. Too dense." He glanced around. "We've had the river water tested several times in the past couple of years and it always tests fine, but for drinking, I prefer the well. It's about as pure as they come."

Gray raised an eyebrow. "Ready for the last leg, or do you need a break?"

"I'm fine." She put her foot in the stirrup and prepared to vault into the saddle, but for some reason the horse spooked, rearing back enough to throw her to the ground.

Marissa lay there for several moments, winded.

She heard Gray's horse thunder near, felt his hands on her shoulders.

"Are you all right? Marissa, what happened?"

She blinked, looked past his shoulder and saw Cody, face paper white, staring at her.

"I'm fine. Just a bit battered." She sat up with his help. "I don't know what happened. One moment she was fine, the next she wasn't." She glanced around. "Where's my horse?"

"She took off. She'll be back. There are cougars in these hills and the horses know it." He helped her up.

"It's not that far to the cabin. We could walk, if you'd like. Or you can ride my horse."

"I'd rather walk." And not have to admit her rear end was sore. She walked beside him, trying to pretend that her head wasn't thudding like a jackhammer.

At the cabin she collapsed into a wicker chair, grateful to be still even if it was temporary. The thudding eased as she stared out over the rippling river. She smiled when a trout flipped up to snatch a fly. The sun's warmth felt stronger in this sheltered valley and she stretched, relishing the feel of it on her skin.

"Here. Drink some of this." Gray's eyes darkened as he watched her sip the cool water from a tin cup.

"It's very refreshing. Thank you." She handed back the cup, her smile fading when he leaned over and pressed his lips against hers. "Wh-what was that for?"

"Just that I'm glad you're back." He grinned, tipped his hat to her.

Cody's giggles drew their attention. His boots and socks had been tossed to one side. Now he sat on a log, trickling his toes through the shallows, pulling his foot out whenever a minnow or something else got too close.

"Aren't you going to say anything?"

Her husband stared at her as if he expected her to do something about that kiss.

But what? She decided to ignore the question.

"Actually, I thought I'd sit here and soak up the sun. It feels good on my sore—that is, my tired muscles." She stretched out her legs, leaned back and closed her eyes, then popped one open. "You will watch him, won't you?"

"You don't have to pretend. I know certain parts must be tender."

She thought it was a joke until she looked up, saw his face.

"Rissa, what happened to your fear of water?"

She blinked.

"I have a fear of water?" That didn't sound right. She peered up at Gray in confusion. "I guess it's gone. I certainly don't feel afraid. Cody can swim, but he still needs to be watched."

She didn't want to answer the questions she knew would come, so she closed her eyes again.

He stood there for a few moments, his feet signaling his impatience as they tromped down the dried grass. After a moment he walked away. A quick peek told her he was with Cody, studying the fish, no doubt.

She closed her eyes again, tried to name all the things she could distinguish. The pungency of overripe cranberries, spruce and pine sap, the musk of sun-dried grasses. And of course, a tiny bite in the air that told her summer was on the wane.

She'd watched spring turn to summer when she'd been with Cody at the cabin. The nights had been cold at first and they'd piled on the thick army blankets *he'd* provided. But gradually the days had lengthened. She'd picked wild strawberries one afternoon, the berries staining Cody's hands and lips. They'd played a game of hide-and-seek. *He* hadn't liked that, was afraid they'd make too much noise. But Cody had coaxed him to join them. It had been fun for a while, until he'd caught on to what she was doing—trying to find someone or something that could help them. He'd tied her up that evening while he and Cody went for supplies.

"Marissa? What's wrong?"

Gray's hand on her shoulder shattered the memories and they dissolved.

"No!" she cried. "Not yet."

"It's okay, sweetheart. You're okay." He lifted her out of the chair, gathered her into his arms and held her against his chest. "You're safe."

And she was, as safe as any woman blessed to be loved by him could be. For once she gave in to her desires, burrowed her head into his neck and simply wrapped her arms around his neck, content to be protected, even though that wasn't what had elicited her yell. She'd wanted to remember her abductor's face, but no matter how hard she searched her brain, it just wasn't there.

Not yet, at least.

"It's not that I'm complaining or anything, but is everything okay?"

She glanced up, met his silver stare mere inches from her nose.

"Yes. I remembered. Not all of it, but a piece. A pretty good-sized piece." She wiggled her way out of his arms, grabbed a stick and began drawing in the dirt. "It was a cabin, a log cabin, homemade, I think. It had a sort of kitchen here with a table and three chairs with shelves behind it. Pots hung here. There was a fireplace, but we mostly cooked outside. This is how the river was situated."

He said nothing, just stood there, watching. Cody watched, too, but as the memories flooded back, Marissa paid neither much heed.

''It was a grove, carved out of the forest. Just like a fairy tale. Maybe it was a hunter's cabin—I don't know. There was an open part here, and we used to sit there in the sun to get warm. When the days got too hot, we had a little awning thing where the wind whistled through off the river and cooled us.''

She told him every single thing that came into her brain, until her voice grew hoarse and she could think of nothing more.

''And the man, Marissa? What did he look like?''

''He was—''

''Ayieeeeeee—'' The strange and heartrending wail came from Cody, his eyes huge as they rested on her. Tears rolled down his cheeks. He shook his head, back and forth, his expression begging her. But for what? To do what? Marissa didn't know.

She felt helpless in the face of his anguish. All she could offer was the same comfort Gray had given her. She gathered his little body into her arms and rocked him back and forth until the last sob died away.

''I can't remember a face, Gray,'' she whispered, staring up at him. ''I want to, so badly. But it's just not there.''

But Gray seemed not to have heard her. His attention was focused completely on his son, who'd drifted off to sleep.

''He knows,'' he whispered. ''Cody knows. I saw it on his face, when you were remembering. He was afraid you'd tell me what the guy looked like.''

''Are you sure?'' She glanced down at her sleeping son.

''I'm sure, Marissa.'' Gray nodded. ''He knows exactly who kidnapped him. But for some reason of his own, he doesn't want to tell us. What we have to do is find out the reason.''

''But how? He doesn't talk.''

''Deliberately, I'm guessing. That way he won't slip up.''

''But that would mean he's shielding the person who abducted us!'' She could hardly give credence to what he was saying. ''Why would he do that?''

''Only Cody knows the answer to that.'' His mouth tightened. ''But if that creep threatened my son in any way, I'll—''

The rest was left unspoken. But Marissa knew what it meant.

She closed her eyes and prayed for a miracle.

Chapter Nine

"It's getting harder for him to remain silent."

The psychologist drew them away from the observation glass, pointed to a battered sofa with ratty cushions.

"If your theory is correct, Gray, then Cody is operating under what is commonly called the Stockholm syndrome. For some reason, he has identified with his captor. So much so that he fears giving him away. Not speaking is his way of avoiding that eventuality."

"You mean it's not that he *can't,* but that he *won't* speak. That's what I thought." Gray pinched his lips together, stemming the anger that some criminal could make his son identify with him. He caught sight of Marissa's face and folded his fingers over Marissa's icy ones, knowing exactly how she felt. "So what comes next?"

"It will be very tricky. You can't ask him outright, because he will only remain silent longer."

"Then how can we help him?" Marissa turned her worried gaze toward Gray.

At least she was sharing this with him, seeing them as parents worried about their child. Her mind had released her that much, for which he told himself to be grateful.

"It's a process, Mrs. McGonigle. It cannot be rushed. It's a matter of Cody knowing he's secure, that he hasn't betrayed or abandoned the person who cared for and protected him out in the bush."

"*I* did that!"

Gray almost chuckled at Marissa's indignation. Talk about a mother bear with her cub!

"I realize that. But this man, whoever he is, has somehow elicited sympathy from Cody, made him feel, um, sort of responsible for his happiness. If you could remember more, we might have a better understanding of how he did that, but as it is..." He shrugged.

"As it is, we have to make Cody realize he belongs with us, that he's a part of our family, that his place is at home. Because we have no idea if he used threats or played on his sympathy or what. Am I right?"

"That's about it."

Last night while Marissa slept, Gray had read everything he could find on the Internet about kidnapping victims and a little about the so-called Stockholm syndrome. He'd remembered the Hearst case and gone from there. What he'd learned had done little to reassure him. The process often took years.

"It sounds like unbrainwashing, if that's a word, after a person's been involved in some cult."

"In a way it is like that, Mrs. McGonigle. I believe

Cody is convinced this man was his dear friend. He also believes he owes it to this person to—if not prevent, then certainly not to assist with his capture. I'm sorry I can't help you more. There's just not enough information, at this point, to go on. You've been to the police?''

''Oh, yes.'' Marissa rolled her eyes. ''Saturday night until the wee hours, and Sunday after church. I thought they were going to move in.''

''They're just trying to help.'' Realizing the interview was at an end, Gray rose and held out a hand to Marissa, who seemed trapped in the sagging sofa.

''Thanks.''

''We appreciate you seeing us on such short notice, Doctor. We'll not take up any more of your time.'' Gray led Marissa to the door.

''It's not a problem. This case is fascinating.'' The doctor studied Marissa, offered a tentative smile. ''I'm sure the memories will return much quicker now that they've started. At least, that's the usual way.''

''But there's nothing usual about anything in this case,'' Marissa murmured under her breath. Aloud she said, ''I know. Thank you.'' She moved off to retrieve Cody.

''She doesn't seem bothered by her own returning memory,'' the doctor mused.

''No, in fact, she wants to go back to the site where they found her, look around. See where the car went over the embankment.'' Gray shrugged his disapproval. ''She thinks it might trigger something else, like the guy's face, though I'm not so sure.''

''May I suggest that you leave Cody behind while

you do this? It would be better if he didn't know how hard you're searching for this person.''

''I don't want to lie to him.'' Gray had never lied to his child, and he wasn't about to start now.

''Of course not. That's not what I'm suggesting. I'm just advising you that he doesn't need to hear everything that you and your wife discuss.''

The doctor's pager beeped. He said goodbye, then hurried away. As Gray watched him stride down the hall, he heard echoes of Miss Blessing's voice from yesterday, reminding him that God was answering his prayers, even though he hadn't specifically prayed. Have faith, she'd said.

But how long could you hold on to that when your arms ached to gather your loved ones close? Had faith brought them back? He didn't know anymore. He only knew that he wasn't the type to sit waiting for God to do something. However futile Miss Winifred found his efforts, he had to do *something*. That was just the way he was—wasn't it?

They left the hospital, dropped Cody at school and drove back to the ranch. For most of the journey Marissa was silent. But when he pulled into the yard and turned off the engine, she remained in her seat.

''Are you okay?''

''No.'' She turned angry blue eyes on him. ''I'm sick of this—sick of little bits of the past floating up so I can skim them off and try to figure out some more of who I am. I'm sick of wondering if I did the right thing, fought as hard as I could have to get Cody away from him, if I was weak or sloppy.''

''I can answer that. You did everything in your

power to keep Cody safe.'' He reached out a hand, touched her cheek. ''And you succeeded.''

''Did I? Then how did he get us, Gray? You said there was no sign that we were forced off the road, so why did I stop? Why didn't he send a ransom note instead of keeping us for all that time?'' Her eyes darkened. ''How could we have found our way home, yet you searched and couldn't find us?'' She clasped her head in her hands. ''None of it makes sense.''

''Marissa—'' He didn't know what to say. She was right, after all. They'd found few answers in these past weeks, and what they had learned had only led to more questions.

''I'm trying to have faith, you know.'' Her tear-laden lashes were thick above her expressive eyes. ''I know God can do anything. I know He's there, that He sees us, that we can depend on Him. I know all that. But I want answers. I want to feel like I'm coming home when I drive into this yard. I want to remember people when they say hello to me on the street.''

Her face was flushed, her skin glowing from the slight sunburn she'd received on their ride to the river cabin. She'd never looked more beautiful to him. Nor more distant.

Why hadn't he found them? Couldn't she have sent some kind of sign, made some gesture that he could have traced? She had to have known he was looking. The questions ate at him like acid. But what good would it do to ask her to answer? She was already frustrated, and who could blame her? She had enough to deal with.

"It'll get better, honey," he murmured, only half believing it himself.

"Will it? When?" She spread her hands, then stared down at her rings. "What if God leaves me like this? What if I never remember how we fell in love, our wedding day, our honeymoon?"

Something inside him screamed a protest. He didn't care if she forgot everything else. She had to remember him. She *had* to.

"I'll help you remember."

"How? What can you do? Show me pictures? It hasn't worked so far."

"Then maybe we need to try something else." He climbed out of the truck, went around to her side and pulled open the door. She climbed out, a frown marring her beautiful face. "Wait here for a minute." He strode across the yard, up the steps and into the house. After a quick conference with Mrs. Biddle, he went back to her, held out a hand.

"Come on."

"Where are we going?"

"You'll see." He led her to the tack room, saddled their horses and helped her mount, refusing to give any more details. Then he led her across his land, over the gullies and streams until they came to the meadow.

Marissa's meadow.

"It's beautiful," she whispered, sliding off her mare, her eyes wide as she took in the field of daisies that still fluttered in the autumn breeze.

"It's yours." Gray stood still, content to watch her reaction.

"Mine?" She strolled through the stalks of flowers that reached to her thighs, breathing in their sweet summer scent. One hand trailed over the white blossoms with their yellow centers. "How could this be mine?"

"I call it Marissa's meadow. I planted it for you."

"You planted it for me?" She stared at him, her head tilted to one side, blue eyes wide with surprise. "It's quite lovely. Thank you."

"This is where I asked you to marry me, Marissa."

Her eyes widened into huge blue circles as she absorbed the information.

There were a thousand things that needed doing on the ranch. Enough work for four men. But Gray stuffed away the guilt that once would have prodded him to go back. This was more important.

He spread the old quilt he'd tucked behind his saddle and patted the area beside him. "Sit down."

She sat, near but not too near, as if she weren't quite certain of his intentions. Swallowing his pride and his nervousness, he told her how he'd planned it all before the snow had melted, ten years ago.

"I had to find enough perennials to fill the meadow. It wasn't easy. I couldn't go to Blessing to get the plants, because people would start asking questions, want to know what I was doing. I wanted to surprise you."

"You've succeeded," she whispered.

He smiled as she fingered the delicate stems of fragile bluebells bending over the edges of the quilt. He could still remember her gasp of delight.

"I came every day, checked to be sure they had enough moisture, that none had died in the transplant. We had decent rains that year and they did well. Then when the whole place was blooming, we came out here for a picnic.''

''And that's when you asked me.'' She peered up at him, then glanced down at her fingers, her knuckle moving automatically to flick the slipping diamond back into place. ''Apparently I must have said yes?''

He nodded, reached for her hand.

''I gave you this ring that day. I was so scared you wouldn't like it, that you'd rather have picked out your own. I even dropped it while I was trying to put it on your finger.''

''But why wouldn't I have liked it? It's a beautiful ring, Gray.'' Her voice grew soft, pensive as she lifted her hand and let the sunlight sparkle against the diamond. ''It looks a bit like a daisy, with its center and these little diamonds, like petals, pushing out from it. Daisies are my favorite. They're so strong, they grow anywhere, but they're delicate, too. They're pretty and functional, and they thrive in their own environment.''

She'd said the same thing that day, he remembered. But he wasn't stuck in the past. He was living, breathing the pure pleasure of having her here, in a place special only to them. She was so close—near enough that he caught the subtle scent of her flowery perfume. Near enough that her arm brushed his. Near enough to kiss.

How could they have lost it all? How could she not remember even a little of what they'd shared? Was it because she didn't want to remember?

No! Gray thrust the notion away, kept his gaze centered on her, here, with him. Within seconds the peace had returned to his soul. He leaned forward, brushed his lips against hers.

To his utter joy she responded, her arms curling around his neck, her fingers tangling in the hair at his nape as she answered him. He took his time, savoring the touch of her soft persuasive lips against his, tangling his hand in the glossy strands of her hair, trailing his fingers down her spine.

''I remember we picked a bouquet to celebrate,'' she murmured, her mouth grazing his jaw, sliding up to his ear. ''I wanted to get married right away. I'd been waiting for you to ask me for so long.'' She initiated the kiss this time, her whole body welcoming his touch.

Delight surged through him. It was like old times, almost. Marissa was here, close enough to hold, to touch, to love. She was his wife, his, and he prized her more than his own life. She made life fun, interesting. Even the drudgery was easy with Marissa waiting for him. In this very place they'd shared their hopes and dreams. He'd shared his dream of having his brother as a partner. In her meadow she'd mourned her mother's death, when the first green sprouts were just beginning to push through the fertile ground. He'd come here after Harris's will had been read. It was in this place that Marissa had told him about their child.

His senses were on fire for this woman. He wanted to do much more than kiss her. But Gray rigidly tamped them down, refused to push her. Marissa had to come to him of her own free will. She had to want him as much as he wanted her. However long that took.

''Um.'' She shifted slightly so that she remained in his arms, but her head rested against his shoulder. Her fingers brushed over his brow, smoothing the creases, but she kept her eyes shadowed. "I like kissing you, Mr. McGonigle. That's a start, isn't it?"

"Yes." He wrapped his arms around her, held her snugly against him while he rested his chin on her head and stared across the flower-strewn meadow. "A very good start, because I like kissing you, too. What else do you remember, Marissa?"

"Well." She closed her eyes, thought for a few minutes. "Something about a notebook?" She blinked up at him. "Is that right?"

He nodded, secretly rejoicing that for now, the floodgates of her mind seemed open.

"You had the tiniest little one in your purse. We planned the wedding in about ten minutes after I proposed. You knew exactly what you wanted. I didn't much care, as long as I didn't have to wait very long." He grinned with smug satisfaction. "I didn't."

"It was a summer wedding, wasn't it? I remember running down the steps. The grass was green and the sky was blue and…rose petals?" She stopped. Confusion shone in her azure eyes as she looked to him for answers.

"Actually it was a beautiful autumn day, sunny, unseasonably warm. Dani was your junior bridesmaid. She thought throwing rose petals was a romantic touch."

"Oh. You mean Luc's wife?" She nodded. "We must have been friends. When we were introduced at church, I felt like I'd known her before. We should invite them over soon."

That was the old Marissa. Fill the house with people. Cast out the pain and shadows of the past with joy and friends. She'd brought light and hope into his life. And he wanted it back.

"Do you remember our honeymoon?" He said it deliberately, watching her face for some sign that she hadn't forgotten that special week.

"Our honey—" Her face flushed a deep hot pink. "No, I don't."

"Are you sure?" He pressed his lips against that sensitive spot on her neck and nibbled gently, mentally begging her to remember.

"Wh-where did we go?" she whispered, her breathing slightly ragged. "Maybe if you told me where—" Her lips opened to his and she fell silent.

"You know, Marissa," Gray whispered several moments later, his hand cupping her defiant chin. "Somewhere inside that brain, you know." He kissed her again, knowing it would take only a word of encouragement from her to send this fire out of control.

"The cabin," she whispered, staring at him. "We went to Dani's cabin."

He froze, letting whatever memories she had found surface. Her eyes changed, widened, grew brighter.

"I caught a fish."

He nodded.

"A huge one."

"Yes. Though I think it's grown some over the years."

He waited, his own mind recalling details he'd forgotten.

"You tipped the canoe on purpose!" She was as indignant now as she'd been back then. "I got soaked."

"You dried."

She frowned at his lazy smile, then blinked.

''Oh.'' Her skin bloomed a rich rosy-red before she tugged herself out of his arms.

His heart sank, but he forced himself not to show it.

''Gray, I can't—''

''I know.'' He rose, pulled her up beside him. ''You're not ready. I understand.'' He brushed a kiss against the end of her nose. ''Don't worry about it, sweetheart. Just let the memories come back as they will. We'll sort it out.''

She was silent while he whistled for the horses, packed up their quilt and handed her a bouquet of daisies. In fact, Marissa said not a word all the way home. She dismounted and removed her own tack, curried her horse as carefully as she always had.

Gray watched, knowing that what she did came from rote memory, not from something that had just occurred. She seemed unaware of what she was doing. As they walked back to the house, he threaded his hand through hers, wondering if the bond he felt with her seemed stronger only to him.

Her next words shocked him back to reality.

''I want to go to where it all began, Gray. I want to see where the car went over. Can we do that?''

He gulped. It had cost him dearly the first time he'd seen it. But Marissa was home. So was Cody. He nodded finally.

''If that's what you want,'' he whispered.

''It is. Maybe it will help,'' she replied, her fingers tightening around his.

Maybe. But he had his doubts.

* * *

Ever since the day in the meadow, Gray had stopped treating her with kid gloves. He kissed her often and thoroughly, sometimes in front of Cody or Mrs. Biddle, sometimes catching her alone. And every time she responded from some place deep inside her that remembered this part of her marriage, thrilling to his touch, to his soft whispers of endearment, to the flickers of yearning his kisses left behind.

Marissa knew she felt something. But was it love—the same love she'd had before? Or was it just some kind of perverse relief that she now knew she'd been married to this man, knew it in her own mind? Was she mistaking love for gratefulness?

Now, as they drove along the highway to the place her nightmare had begun, she ignored the questions. She was simply glad he was there. If something happened, he'd help her get through it.

She'd expected a flash of illumination, a stab of pain, anger, helplessness. Something. But when Gray pulled to the side and showed her the place where her car had gone off the road and tumbled down an embankment, she saw, felt nothing. It was as if it had happened to someone else.

''Nothing?''

She didn't want to answer, hated to see the despair flood his eyes at yet another disappointment.

''Maybe if we walked down the embankment?''

He knew it was pointless, that according to the police theory she and Cody had been removed from the vehicle before it ever went over. But at least she was making some effort to push back the curtain. Was it because she wanted their marriage back, too?

He took her hand as they half slipped, half walked

down the steep incline, the undergrowth slick from last night's rain. Partway down she had to stop him.

"Let's go back."

He stared at her, then turned wordlessly and began climbing back up.

"I'm sorry, Gray."

"It's not your fault." He forced a smile, brushed his knuckles against her cheek, then took the hand she stretched out toward him, but his face was granite. Once more she was a disappointment to him. And it hurt.

The drizzle that had fallen all morning began anew. They hurried back to their own vehicle, neither one speaking. What was there to talk about?

The question that had been hanging at the back of her brain for days pushed forward. She'd told herself not to ask it, but they had nothing else to go on. No more leads to follow up, nothing but one single road to whatever had happened in the past. Did she have courage enough to tread that road? To hear the truth?

She peered through the mist-covered windshield, watched the wipers stroke back and forth as the hills flew past. Finally she mustered the courage.

"Gray, what did we argue about that last day?"

If she hadn't been watching him, she'd have missed the fractional tightening of his mouth, the quick, furtive glance he gave her.

"It doesn't matter. It won't help you remember, Marissa."

"You don't know that." She scrambled to make him understand. "From that first day I woke up in the hospital, it's been there, hanging over me like a big black question mark. Was I angry and perhaps driving too fast? Did I not pay enough attention to road conditions? Had I stopped at the side of the road because I intended to turn around?'' She laid a hand on his arm, pleaded with him. ''Please tell me. It might help, Gray.''

''It won't.'' Lips clamped together, he said nothing else for several miles.

''You don't know that.'' She fought back tears to try to make him understand. ''I've come to a dead end. There's nothing else I can think of that might help. I need something to go on. Please?''

He sighed. They were on the graveled stretch of road now, heading for home. He pulled to a stop, then began to speak.

''It was about Adam. Back then it was always about Adam.''

''I don't understand.''

''It goes back a long way, Marissa, long before us.'' He glanced sideways at her, then continued. ''Remember that Dani's father bought a piece of land from my father, which was apparently never paid for? The only notation I could find in the ledgers was 'Fancy Dancer.' I figured it was a horse they'd traded, but it could never have covered the cost of such a big piece of land. I figured Dermot DeWitt, Dani's father, had welshed on their deal, which is why my father and hers had a falling-out.''

''But Dani's your friend.''

He nodded.

''I hope so. I never said anything after I found out about the land, because by then Dani was fighting to hang on to the ranch and I didn't want to add to her misery.''

"She didn't know where it came from?"

"No, but later, after reading her father's diary, she found out and insisted on paying me for it, as much as she could. We set up a rental system. I used her land for a fee, which she pays back to me as interest on the loan. I didn't like it, but she wouldn't have it any other way. She's pretty proud."

"Good for her." But this didn't explain what she and Gray had argued about. "Go on."

"The original idea was for Adam to ranch the land, but then he hurt his back calf roping. I figured he could at least help with the book work, even if he couldn't actively ranch, but he wouldn't do it. Kept saying I'd stolen it from him, and now I could drown trying to keep it going. We had a huge argument. Both of us said stuff we shouldn't have. He took off." He cleared his throat. "You were furious when you found out the next morning. Told me I had the wrong end of the stick, that I was trying to punish Adam by forcing him to do what I wanted, instead of listening to what he wanted."

"Were you?"

He raked a hand through his hair.

"The truth is, I don't know anymore, Rissa. I guess I did have some kind of plan in my mind—I figured we'd ranch together, build Harris's spread into something really big, you know, brothers working side by side." He made a face. "I was a fool to think it. It had never been like that before. Why did I expect everything to change? Adam's never been able to accept me as Harris's son."

She couldn't bear the hurt on his face and moved across the seat to hug him.

"At least you tried."

"Yeah, I did. But Adam couldn't get past the fact that he'd been cut out, left a pile of money instead of the land he figured was his birthright." He sighed. "He had a right to be upset. I wasn't the rightful son. Not really. Harris had a one-night stand with my mother. Before she died, Mom told me she'd wanted to tell him until she found out that he was already married to someone else. She refused to do anything that would ruin his marriage, so she pushed herself to provide for me. She tried hard, but we never had much. Eventually it wore her down and she got sick. Let's just say it wasn't a fairy-tale childhood."

"I'm sorry." Marissa knew the memories were hard on him. He'd spoken before about his rough childhood, his insistence that Cody would never experience the same thing.

"So am I. But in spite of our rough life, I had the one thing Adam apparently didn't. I knew my mother loved me." He sighed, rubbed his chin. "After her death I found a letter telling me who my father was. In it she begged me to go and see him. I did, but I signed on as a hand. I'd only been there a couple of days when Harris called me in. 'You're Leslie's son,' he said. I never knew how he found out, but from then on I was his son, equal with Adam in everything."

"Until the will."

"Yeah." He leaned toward her, his silvery gaze intent. "I would have walked out a long time ago, but I'd made him a promise that I wouldn't let his ranch die. I couldn't break my word. Besides, we had Cody. This was his home. I couldn't sell the place, because of my promise. The only thing I could do was work it. I made sure Adam got half of everything, but it wasn't enough. He'd decided to hate me and he took every chance he could to let me know."

"But why?"

"I never knew. At least, not until lately." He frowned, his hand brushing her hair in soft, even strokes. "Adam thinks he wasn't really Harris's son, that his mother lied about it so he'd inherit the ranch."

"What do you think?"

"I didn't know her. She'd left years before I came along. But Harris wasn't a fool. Nobody could have pulled one over on him. I know he did some paternity tests. I'm going to go back through his papers, see if I can find something that will prove to Adam that he was Harris's child."

"Good." She sat there watching the rain fall harder, obliterating the land as their breath created a mist on the inside of the windshield. This man she had married had a big heart. He'd go above and beyond to make sure a man who claimed to hate him wouldn't suffer because of something that might not be true.

Gray kept ranching because he'd promised his father. He'd done his mother's bidding, though that must have cost him, too.

How could she not love Gray McGonigle?

And yet something, some prickle of worry about the past, kept her from accepting it, from telling him.

"I guess I've skirted the question long enough. You wanted to know what we argued about."

At last! Now maybe she could break through that black wall.

"Yes. Please."

His hands tightened around her as if he were afraid, once she'd heard him out, she'd try to get away.

''Don't hate me, Marissa,'' he begged, his voice a tortured whisper.

''Of course I won't hate you.'' She reached out, touched his lips with her fingertips. ''But isn't it better to get it all out, to have the truth and deal with it? No more secrets, Gray.'' She saw him lift one eyebrow and grinned. ''Well, not intentional ones, anyway.''

He kissed her hard, as if he needed that embrace to give him courage. Then he set her away and began speaking.

''It's funny you should mention secrets today. Back then—well, you'd been very mysterious. When I asked, all you would say was that you were checking into something, that you were very close to finding out the truth.''

''The truth about what?''

He shrugged.

''I don't know. But that day, just before you left for work, I had a phone call from someone who told me that Adam was using the ranch to back personal loans he was making. I was furious. I knew by then that it wasn't going to work for us to be partners and I decided I'd tell him to leave. He was using his back injury to hang around, drawing a salary but not contributing. We were strapped financially, you were working and had put Cody in school to do it, and I felt guilty that I couldn't provide enough. I'd had it with his blame and anger and constant harping about me stealing his birthright. I wanted him out of our lives.''

''We argued about Adam?'' She didn't understand.

"You asked me, no, begged me not to do anything about it until you got home that evening. You said you'd explain it all, that there was no need for anyone to leave, that Harris had meant for both of us to share his legacy." He frowned. "You were so adamant about it that I finally agreed to wait."

"Then—"

"I went out to the barn after you left. I'd bought Dani's best breeding stock to help her pay off the ranch. I couldn't afford it, things were already pretty tight for us, but—"

"You wanted to help." She understood that much.

"Anyway, Adam was there loading a horse, the best stallion, into a truck. He'd arranged for it to go as payment in a card game he'd lost. As if that animal were his! I was furious. I told him he'd have to pay off his own debts from then on, that Harris was right not to leave him the ranch, that he was a shame and embarrassment to his father's memory."

"Oh, Gray." Tears welled as she realized the depth of pain both men had endured.

"We argued, he left. By then it was too late to take it back." He was silent for a moment, remembering. "You phoned just before leaving work to pick up Cody. You were so excited, said you'd found something that would explain a lot. You asked me to make sure Adam was there when you got home. I told you what I'd done. You blew up, said it was all needless. That Adam had as much right to the land as I did."

He looked at her, his face sad.

"I said some terrible things, Marissa. Accused you of stuff I knew you'd never do. And you hung up on me."

"What things?" She knew he didn't want to repeat it, that it hurt him just to think about it. But wounds festered unless they were cauterized. It was better to get it all out, then let it seep away.

"I said you'd always taken Adam's part, that you seemed to care more about him than you ever had about me. I—I asked you why you didn't just pack up and go with him, if you were so determined to make sure he was all right."

"Gray!" She gaped, shocked by his words.

"That isn't the worst of it." He swallowed hard, his Adam's apple bobbing up and down. "I—I said that if you wanted to leave, that was perfectly fine by me, that I could soon find someone else. I—I told you to go, but said that you had to drop Cody off first. You could do what you wanted, but Cody was my son and no one else was going to raise him."

She stared at him, knowing the bitter words had sprung from a wellspring of emotions that had been tamped down over time, that frustration and anger and disappointment had all played a part. But the knowledge that he'd actually told her to leave… It hurt.

"You never said anything for the longest time. Then in this soft quiet voice you whispered, 'Goodbye, Gray,' and hung up. That afternoon you disappeared and I knew that I'd ruined everything. Poetic justice, don't you think?"

It was as if Marissa had backtracked in time, to that first morning when she'd awakened with that black yawning gap in her head. Only, this was worse, infinitely worse. Because she knew now that she'd cared about him, that he'd loved her. Once. She'd seen glimpses of their past, of the love that had bound them together, made them a team, pushing for the same goal. But to let her go so easily…

Was that why she couldn't quite bring herself to actually say the words that day in the meadow? Had she stopped loving Gray on that forgotten day more than five months ago? Had she really been leaving him, taking away his son? Maybe he had found someone else, someone who could help him with the ranch, someone who knew what he was talking about when he tried to discuss his work with them.

Perhaps that wonderful love she'd believed they'd shared was really nothing more than a mirage, a shimmering wish her brain had created because it couldn't deal with the truth—that their marriage was over.

She realized that her hand was aching and looked down. Gray had hold of it, was squeezing it tightly as he watched her.

"Rissa, please don't hate me. I didn't mean it! I was angry and I said a lot of stupid things. But I love you. I always have. There isn't anyone else. There could never be anybody but you." He loosened his fingers, closed them around her arm. "I never wanted you to leave. Never."

Never wanted *her* to leave, or was it Cody he was afraid of losing?

"I have to go inside now," she whispered, shifting away from him to open her door. "I have to think."

"Marissa—"

She slammed the door on the rest of his words.

And on the hope she'd been clinging to for so long.

This time Gray couldn't blame God.

Chapter Ten

"Fine," Gray repeated for what felt like the hundredth time. "Everything is just fine. Thank you."

Except it wasn't.

Oh, no one would notice anything just by looking at them. Marissa made certain of that. But away from the church and the people who'd known her so well, out of the spotlight, that glittering smile dissipated and she withdrew into the out-of-reach shell she'd created.

Even Cody had noticed, though Gray wouldn't believe Marissa intended him to be touched by their problems. But perhaps because of his refusal to speak, Cody had become more perceptive to the atmosphere and other people's feelings. Last night after dinner, while Marissa had sat staring into the fire, he'd approached her, and when she didn't immediately reach for him, Cody had laid his head on her knee, his fingers touching her face, silently sharing her pain.

It hurt, burned deeper than any branding iron ever could to know that he'd lost her for the second time.

Suddenly all Gray wanted was to get out of this church, away from all the comments about God giving them a miracle. This wasn't a miracle. This was a nightmare, only he couldn't wake up.

"I'll be outside when you're ready to leave," he whispered in her ear, then eased past her friends to stride out into the cold northern wind that would soon bring winter. The land was bleak now, barren, like his soul.

"Still fighting God?" Winifred Blessing stood behind him, her eyes brimming with sympathy. "Oh, Gray, you make it so hard on yourself."

He did not want to hear this.

"Can I do anything to help?"

"I don't think anyone can do anything to fix things, but thanks for asking, Miss Winifred." He kept his face averted, stared into the open spaces beyond Blessing township. Colorado was a big place—there was plenty of opportunity to be had. But since the day Harris had claimed him as son, he'd never wanted to be anywhere but here, working the ranch.

Today, now, he'd gladly hand it over and walk away without a single regret, if he could just have another chance to make his marriage work, to have Marissa love him again.

"You told her about that last day, didn't you?"

He wheeled around, staring at her.

"How did you—"

"She stopped by to see me that day, you know. She told me what you'd said." Miss Blessing shook her head. "It's the only thing that makes sense now. You two were getting along so well. Only something like telling her about that day could have caused those doubts.''

''Doubts?'' He was only half listening to what she said, his eye following Cody as he walked to the edge of the ravine behind the church, to the exact spot where he'd been found, and stood there, staring down.

''Grayson McGonigle, what have you done to show that woman you love her?''

''I told her all the time.'' He frowned at the indignant baker. ''Marissa knew I loved her, Miss Blessing.''

''*Then,* yes. But I'm talking about *today.* What did you do yesterday or today to show her that you love her? Not the words, *actions.*'' She squinted, the bright sunlight highlighting the silver streaks through her golden-blond waves. ''Don't you have an anniversary coming up soon?''

He blinked, glanced at his watch.

October tenth. Less than a week away.

''Actions speak louder than words, Grayson. Maybe it's time you showed her, instead of talking.''

''I've been trying,'' he muttered.

''Try harder. This isn't a crossword puzzle you can put down and come back to later. This is your marriage. Maybe it's time you asked for help from Someone who's in the business of fixing things.''

God, she meant. Ask God for help?

''I had one of my cookies for you, but I'm afraid it got broken and one of Joshua's girls fed it to that ridiculous dog. Still, the message is as apropos as it ever was.''

Oh, no! She was going to give him more advice—which she'd then claim came from God.

"I don't think—"

"Good. Don't think. Just listen. 'Even though a marriage is made in heaven, the maintenance work has to be done here on earth.'"

Meaning what? That he'd taken Marissa and their marriage for granted? She wasn't telling him anything he didn't already know.

"Maintenance work isn't pretty, son. It's the grunt stuff, the day-to-day little routine things that make a world of difference to the big picture. Every morning when I get to work, Furley has the coffee on. She doesn't have to do it. She doesn't even drink the stuff. But it means the world to me to walk in and smell that aroma and know I'll soon be sipping it."

Furley Bowes had been Winifred's bakery assistant for as long as anyone in Blessing could remember. The two had worked as a team for so long, everyone expected to see them together.

"The little stuff, the maintenance. Maybe that's what you need to concentrate on. Ask Him where to start." Having said her piece, Miss Blessing stomped across the grass, pausing to encourage those people God had directed her to.

Gray turned away, frustrated by her unasked-for advice. She was always dishing it out. She'd never been married, never had a child, though she'd raised Joshua Darling after his parents died. But still, what did she know about how things like this worked? He couldn't just barrel up to Marissa and insist she forget the ugliness of his last words. And politely saying "please" and "thank you" wasn't going to cut it. Not in this case.

He walked across the lawn, found a boulder warmed

by the sun and sank onto it, his eyes riveted on Cody, who remained staring into the ravine.

Ask God for help? How could he when it was his own stupidity that had caused the problem? God didn't go around bailing people out of quagmires they'd created for themselves. He helped those who couldn't help themselves. Gray was a man, he was strong, he shouldn't have to depend on someone else.

And yet…

Marissa emerged from the church at that moment. Gray rose, thrust away his uncomfortable thoughts.

"Come on, Cody. Time to go."

The little boy jerked as if he'd been asleep. Slowly he turned from his scrutiny of the steep valley below and walked toward Gray, kicking at the gravel pebbles with his feet. He stood in front of him, staring up, until finally he reached up one hand to snuggle it inside his dad's.

"What's wrong, son?" Gray hunkered down, looked him in the eye. "Were you remembering the day we found you?"

The brown head jerked once in a nod.

"Aren't you glad to be home?"

Cody nodded, but his face wrinkled, as if he were dealing with a huge problem.

"I wish you'd talk to me, tell me what's bothering you. I love you and I want you to be happy. But how can I help you if you won't tell me what's wrong?"

One single tear welled, trembling on the end of his lashes as he stared into Gray's eyes.

"I would never do anything to hurt you or your mom. You know that, don't you?" He watched the nod and heaved a sigh of frustration. "I wish you'd trust me."

At that moment he was glad Miss Blessing had moved on. She'd raise one of those bushy eyebrows and tell him God wished he'd do the same. Gray could almost hear her saying those exact words.

Holding Cody's hand, he walked with his son toward his truck and the woman who waited there, the woman who seemed a stranger.

Later, after they'd shared a quiet lunch, he saw Cody go outside. Gray followed, sinking onto a chair on the veranda as he watched the boy desultorily throw a stick for the dog, kick a ball around the yard.

"He's upset about something." Marissa sank into the chair beside him, her forehead furrowed. "And now Mrs. Biddle has to leave."

"Why?"

"I don't know. She had a phone call before church. I saw her talking to Miss Blessing before the service. Just now she asked if I thought I could manage on my own for a few days. A family emergency, she said."

"Does she need a ride somewhere?"

"I asked her that. She said Winifred is driving her." Marissa didn't look at him. She sat there curled into the farthest corner of the chair, as if she thought he might bite if she got too near.

It stung, but he tamped down his frustration. It was his own fault she was wary. He was lucky she was still talking to him at all.

"Wonder what it's all about."

"I don't know, but she's fairly upset. She phoned someone a while ago. I heard her asking them why she hadn't been notified. I hope it's not serious, but I don't like to ask too many questions.'' Marissa shrugged, huddling into the warmth of her big bulky sweater. ''I guess she'll tell us when she wants us to know.''

''Can you manage on your own?''

''Of course.'' She raised her eyebrows. ''I've been spoiled and coddled with her here. I'm perfectly capable of running my own house.''

Her own house? Well, at least she was staying. For now.

The ringing of the phone broke into their thoughts.

''I'll get it.'' Marissa went inside, returned a few seconds later. ''It's for you. Jake Crabtree?'' She looked puzzled by the name.

Gray stood, tamped down the anticipation that hiked his nerves up a notch. The man probably wanted to be paid, that was all. No reason to get worked up about it.

''Hello, Jake.''

''I found something.'' Never one to bother with convention, Jake launched into the reason for his call. ''A cabin, way in the backwoods. You want to take a look?''

''Yes.'' At last! Maybe now they'd find some answers.

''Tomorrow morning suit you?''

''This afternoon suits me better.''

''No can do. Takes a long time to make the trek back there. I reckon you'll need a full day to hike in, take a look and get back out.''

''Fine. Just tell me where and when.'' He scribbled the details down, agreed on a time, then hung up.

''Gray? Who was that?''

"An investigator I hired. He thinks he's found the cabin where you were held. I need to call the police."

The rest of the afternoon was spent with various members of law enforcement coming and going. Cody sat in the corner and watched it all without saying a word, but there was an expression on his face that bothered Gray. His little face was pinched with worry, as if he was afraid they'd find something tomorrow.

Some*thing* or some*one?* Just how long did this Stockholm syndrome last? And where was Adam? He hadn't seen his brother for several days, though he'd promised to stick around the ranch and watch out for Marissa.

That was Adam for you. Totally undependable. Once more Gray felt the press of responsibility for protecting his family from some unknown danger and from the problems Adam inevitably brought.

When the last person left just before six, Marissa set the table and served their meal, a succulent stew with golden-brown biscuits and fresh peaches for dessert.

Cody ate almost nothing.

"You love peaches, honey. Why not have a few?"

But he shook his head and climbed down from the table. Moments later they heard him moving in his room upstairs.

Gray sat silently, watching as Marissa cleared the table. He helped her store the leftovers and wiped off the place mats, grinning at her surprised look.

"I'm completely domesticated," he told her. "When you had Cody I—" He stopped, coughed. "Never mind."

But Marissa was smiling.

"Oh, I think I need to hear this," she teased. "You cook? Clean? Do laundry? Bathrooms?"

With each question he nodded, until her eyes sparkled with fun.

"I can't imagine it."

"I'd rather ranch," he admitted, which sent her into paroxysms of laughter.

"I'll bet you would."

It was the first time she'd laughed, really laughed, in days. And he wanted it to go on. Forever. He touched her arm gently.

"Marissa, I—"

She pulled her arm from beneath his fingers, her breath catching in her throat.

"No! I need time, Gray. Time to understand, time to think things through. I'm trying, but it's going to take me a while to digest everything. Those words—they aren't easy to forget." She smiled, but it was a sad effort. "That's funny, isn't it? Coming from me, I mean. The great forgetter." She sighed.

He wished it was different, that she'd lean on him, let him soothe away the worries. But he'd ruined that. Now all he could do was stand here and listen to whatever she wanted to share.

"What I'm trying to say is that I—well, I had this vision, a sort of picture of our marriage. Rather childish of me, I suppose, but it kind of helped me get a handle on you, this place, our past life together. And then, well, I had no idea you suspected me of—"

"I didn't." He couldn't let her say the ugly word. "I was mad that you couldn't or wouldn't see only my side of it, that you were always championing Adam. I'm the one who was childish. I wanted my wife supporting me and no one else. I refused to accept that you were trying to help us, trying to prevent me from sending him away permanently.''

The lines of strain eased, if only fractionally, as she listened to him.

''I don't think it was all your fault, you know,'' she whispered. ''If you thought I was always on his side, I must have been doing something wrong.''

''Peacemaking, that's what you were trying to do. You didn't want any irreparable mistakes, and I was on the verge of making one.''

She rubbed her temples.

''I don't know about back then, but I do wish the two of you could find some sort of common meeting ground now. He's your brother, your family. That's more important than any piece of land or a few animals.''

''Believe me, I'm beginning to understand that very well.''

He waited, but Marissa said no more. Instead she sat staring over the rolling hills, reminding him of a Scripture verse.

''I will lift up my eyes to the hills, where my help comes from.''

Is that where they'd find help? Would God ever get around to sorting out this mess? If He did, Gray decided he'd better be certain his own slate was clean, that whatever he'd said in the past, she would know the truth.

He moved, knelt in front of her. He wrapped his fingers around hers.

''I love you, Marissa. I know I never said it enough, or spent enough time showing you. But I did. And do.'' He waited, but she merely nodded. ''Can you—do you think you'll ever be able to forgive me?''

''I can't answer that, Gray.''

''Why not?'' Lord, he was sick of not knowing when this would be over, when he would be on solid ground once more. ''It's a simple question. You must know what your feelings are.''

''That's just it—I don't.'' She glared at him, her eyes turbulent with emotions she wouldn't share. ''How can I say I forgive you? It doesn't feel like it was me you said that to. I mean, I hate it that you said it, but it wasn't to me. Don't you understand? I'm not her.''

The frustration overwhelmed her. Tears rolled down her face.

He couldn't bear to hear it, couldn't bear to see her suffer because of him, or to hear that she didn't want to be married to him anymore. That was the one fear he'd never allowed to take root. He wouldn't now.

''You might as well face it. Whoever I am, I'm not your wife, Gray McGonigle. I just look like her.''

''Don't say that. Yes, you are, Marissa! Deep inside your heart, you know it. It's just taking your brain a while to catch up.'' He grasped her by the upper arms, ignoring her tenseness. ''I love you, darling. Somewhere behind the shadows and the fear and the worry you know that. It's why you came back home.''

He brushed one hand over her hair, forced himself to relax.

''I don't care how long it takes for you to remember. I've got time. I'll wait for you as long as you need me to. Because without you, I'm dead, Marissa. You and Cody, you make my life worthwhile. We share something very special, a history together that nobody and nothing can ever erase. Not even my stupidity. You belong here. Okay?''

She studied him for a long time, her blue eyes darker now with secrets she didn't explain. Finally she spoke, softly, hesitantly.

''I don't know if I belong here, Gray. Not yet. But let me find my own way through this. I have to do this in my own time. Okay?''

He nodded. But inside his heart was screaming—hurry!

Hurry!

The night was dark, cold, a hint of frost in the air.

He eased open the patio door Brett had said he'd leave unlocked and stepped inside, sniffing. Someone had been baking and the aroma was tantalizing. He stole into the kitchen, saw the cake and cut himself a piece, carefully eating it over the sink so he could push the crumbs down the drain.

He was tired of living out of cans with nobody to talk to but himself. He wanted Brett to come back so they could play. He liked the fishing game best, but only if Brett was there. *She* couldn't come. Not this time. She made good things to eat, and she'd been nice to him, but she'd taken Brett away. That was bad. Because Brett was his.

He turned on the tap, just a trickle to wash his hands, then dried them on a paper towel that he tucked into his pocket. There was a picture on the fridge and he stared at it. It was *her.* She had her arm around Brett. That made him mad. He saw a pair of scissors sitting in a wooden block on the counter and he picked them up.

She couldn't have Brett. Not ever.

He cut around her, freeing Brett. Now he would take it home, put it with his other picture at the cabin. Tomorrow he'd go back to that little grocery store and stock up for when Brett came. It would be soon, he knew that. Brett liked the cabin and the little bunk bed he'd made especially for him.

But he had hardly any money. How would he be able to get enough cans for a whole winter? He pulled open a long cupboard door, peered inside. Most of the things weren't in cans and he didn't know how to use them. He looked on all the shelves, trying to find enough of the things he liked, but there weren't many cans on these shelves. Maybe *she* didn't use cans here.

At the very bottom of the cupboard he saw something sparkly. He bent down, pulled it out. It was a present. He knew about presents. Presents were for birthday parties and for Christmas. The sparkly paper had birthday cakes all over it and it looked as if the candles were lit. Who was having a birthday?

He turned the package over, saw the card with a little boy and a dog. They were going fishing. It was the kind of card you gave a boy.

Brett was going to have a birthday? He thought of all the ways they could celebrate. Then he remembered—*her*. She wouldn't invite him to the birthday. She didn't like him. She didn't even know Brett's name.

He got mad thinking about her. She wasn't going to have a birthday party for Brett—he was. He tore a hole in the paper, lifted out a remote control truck. It was a stupid gift. Brett didn't care about trucks. He liked animals and the woods and swimming. He liked catching fireflies and frogs and fish. He didn't care about trucks. Not Brett.

She was trying to get Brett away from him. That's what she wanted. To keep them apart by giving Brett things he didn't have at the cabin. In one movement he lifted his heavy boot and squashed the truck.

It made a noise and broken parts flew everywhere. He pushed what he could back under the bottom shelf and put the paper on top to cover it. It wasn't nice to break other people's things, but she shouldn't have done it.

He listened for a long time, but nobody came downstairs to see what the noise was, and finally he felt safe. Then he remembered about the food. How could he have a birthday party for Brett if he didn't have food? Winters were cold. They'd needs lots of cans.

But he had no money. How could he get money? There wasn't any in this cupboard. He'd have to go upstairs and ask Brett. He had to have everything ready.

The stairs were the creaky kind he'd grown up with, so he walked only on the outside parts. He didn't know which room Brett was in, but then he saw a little light and remembered that Brett liked to see some light when he went to sleep. He slipped into that room.

Sure enough, there was his bestest friend, sleeping on his bed. Brett was holding the little glass horse in one hand. They'd had a lot of fun with that horse. But Brett should share. He reached out to take the horse, but Brett woke up and moved his hand away.

That was okay. They could share at the cabin. Then Brett would let him take a turn playing with the horse.

He smiled at the boy, loving the way his dark hair flopped over one eye, as if it was playing peekaboo.

"I'm getting the cabin ready, Brett," he whispered, so softly the little boy had to lean forward to hear. "Pretty soon you'll come and stay, won't you?"

Brett slowly nodded.

"But I have to get some food for us. I need money." He watched the boy slide out of bed. "Quiet, now. Don't wake *her* up. She can't come this time. It's going to be just us. Won't that be fun?"

Brett blinked, nodded, then turned and lifted something off a shelf. There was the tiny jingle that money made. He grinned.

"Good boy, Brett. Now I can get us lots of food. Enough for a long time."

Brett pointed to the door.

"I know. I have to go now. Before *she* wakes up. You won't tell her, will you?" Brett shook his head. "Good. I knew you wouldn't. You're my special boy, Brett. My very special boy. I love you, Brett." He reached down and hugged him as tightly as he could with the jar of money in his arm. Brett hugged him back.

"You get your things ready and I'll come and get you as soon as I can. Okay, Brett?"

The boy nodded.

"Bye, Brett." Brett waved, followed him out into the hall.

He didn't want to go, but if *she* saw him, she'd make a fuss. That's the way she was, because she didn't understand. She'd tried to take Brett away. She thought she could run and run in the forest and he wouldn't find her. But that didn't work because Brett was his boy. He would always find Brett.

He walked back down the stairs, took some cookies from a big glass jar and went to the door where he'd left his shoes. He remembered to click the lock first, then stepped outside and pulled the door closed. The dog ran over to sniff his pocket, but he wouldn't share the cookies. It was a good dog—it hadn't barked or anything—but he still wasn't going to share. He was hungry and it was a long way to the next town.

He was used to walking now. He liked the dark, liked knowing nobody could see him. He'd made a path through the bush, a shortcut that only he knew about. He stopped along the way to take the money out of Brett's jar. It was a heavy jar and he was tired of carrying it. He hid it under a big stone that sometimes got hot when the sun shone on it. He'd come back for Brett's jar sometime, take it back to his house so nobody would notice that it was gone. He didn't want them to know that Brett was helping him.

The sun was just waking up when he decided to rest. The store wouldn't be open for a while. There was time for him to have a sleep if he wanted, and he felt a little bit tired, so why not? He made himself a soft place on the ground in between some bushes, and sprawled out on the nice-smelling pine boughs. He had two cookies left, and he munched on these while he watched God paint the sky.

His mama had told him about God a long time ago, how He watched out for His children. Mama wouldn't like him sleeping outside. She said camping was for people who didn't have a nice soft bed. But if he could just see her, he could explain about Brett.

But Mama was gone. It was his fault, he knew that. He'd been bad. But he hadn't wanted her to go. Not forever. Not like—

No, he didn't want to think about that. Everything got all mixed up when he thought about that bad time. He'd think about God instead. How many paint pots did God need to get the sky all pink and red and blue with orange streaks? His picture was like that—all kinds of colors that mixed together.

After a while he felt better. Mama would understand. After all, she'd loved Brett, too.

Chapter Eleven

It took only a few hours to reach the cabin thanks to the all-terrain bikes the police provided. Noting their early arrival, Marissa couldn't decide whether they were as eager as her to see the site, or whether they were simply tired of looking for clues that never appeared. With all the rain yesterday, Gray had refused to make the trek, but the police had had a team go into the area and, thanks to them, the passage through the bush wasn't nearly as rough as she'd expected.

They'd decided to take Cody along. For one thing because he'd seen the police coming and going, heard what they'd had to say. But for another because Marissa wanted to take away some of the sting seeing the place again might engender. She pretended it was an excursion and Cody had joined in by insisting he would ride behind Jake.

"Does it look familiar?" Gray helped her off the bike, watching closely as she scanned the little clearing.

Whatever Marissa had expected, it wasn't this. Her mind stayed blank, offering no clue, no hint of her inexplicable past. She glanced at Cody behind Jake. He seemed frozen, his body tense, eyes huge as he peeked first right, then left.

She walked across to him, anxious to allay his fears.

"There's no one here, honey," she murmured, kneeling in front of him to clasp her hands around his. "You don't have to be afraid. Nothing's going to happen."

But either he didn't believe her, or he knew something she didn't. Whatever the reason, Cody didn't lose his fearful look. He lifted his precious glass horse from his pocket, then stepped away, putting a distance between them.

She rose, nodded to the sheriff who'd asked her to look around. Nothing looked familiar, but she had to at least make an effort, though all she really wanted was to get out of here, back to the safety of the ranch. She was glad Gray stuck nearby.

"That must be the river I remembered that first day in the hospital," she whispered to him. "Funny. The water doesn't seem as deep."

"You were here in the spring, Marissa. It's always higher then from runoff. It's drained away now." The words were an automatic response. Gray was obviously busy with his own thoughts. He strode across the compound, as if he were looking for something. After a moment he asked for a pair of binoculars.

Marissa followed more slowly, absorbing each thing she happened upon. There was a hearth of river stones, where many fires had burned them black with soot. The ash had been cleaned away, leaving no hint of what had been burned in the center. A neat pile of cleaned-out cans had been formed into some kind of crude shiny silver sculpture. Cody blew on it and made it tinkle, over and over again.

"No fingerprints," Jake told her. "They checked."

After a few minutes, the noise of the cans thrummed through Marissa's head. She felt the fingers of panic inching their way up her spine, matching the beat of the banging cans.

"That's enough, Cody. Let's go inside."

He hung back, his hand dragging against hers. But Marissa's curiosity now had the better of her. She needed to see what was in there. She let go of his hand, took a deep breath and stepped inside, unsurprised when she saw the roughly hewn table, two stools, a small window, bunk beds. Did that mean she knew this place, that she'd been here? Or did it mean that the inside of this place held no fear for her?

If this truly was the place they'd been held, then why couldn't she remember it?

Cody stepped in front of her, reached under the bunk and pulled out a small pair of moccasins, the initials *B R* lettered in blue and white beads across the top. He fingered them gently, rubbing his thumbs against the worn suede, a tiny smile curving his lips.

"May I see?" Marissa hunkered down beside him, staring at the footwear. There was something about the leather—she slid her fingertips across it, then remembered that day in the tack room when she'd been holding the sleeve of Gray's coat. The textures were exactly the same.

"I wonder whose initials these are?"

Cody frowned.

''Did I have a pair of these slippers, honey?''

He shook his head, took them from her, then carefully replaced the footwear underneath the cot where he'd found them. He straightened, grabbed her hand and pulled, as if he was in a hurry to leave.

''So I wasn't wearing anything on my feet, which is why they were tanned, and not my legs.''

She headed for the door, then noticed something under the table. She walked over, pulled out a chair and saw the painting she'd done of Cody sitting on it.

''It's yours, isn't it?'' The sheriff watched her.

Marissa nodded.

''I left it outside to dry after I finished. There was a storm and when I went to get it, it was gone.'' She brushed one finger over the colors that had washed down. ''Someone got it wet.''

''The bunks are the same?''

She nodded. ''Me on top, Cody below.''

''Where did your abductor sleep?''

She frowned, glanced around the room.

''I don't know. Not in here, I don't think.'' She saw the skepticism darken his eyes. ''I can't really remember.'' She closed her eyes, tried to remember.

''Anything else?''

''There were some pots, a few dishes. Chipped, mismatched, like something you'd get at a secondhand or thrift store.''

''Nothing like that here, Sheriff.''

Since there was nothing else to see in the tiny room, Marissa followed Cody out. The sparsity of the conditions shocked her. How had they survived here for almost half a year?

She caught a glimpse of Gray speaking to an officer

and walked toward them, noting the lines of strain that pulled her husband's mouth down. She might not remember a lot, but that expression she knew. He was furious about something.

"What's wrong?"

"I know this place."

Nothing could have prepared her for that. Marissa froze, her body radar zipping to a high state of alert.

"Wh-what do you mean? How could you know it?" She stared at him, unable to believe what he'd just said. "Do you mean you've been here before?"

He nodded.

"I'm pretty sure we're on my land. Years ago Adam showed me this cabin after we'd come out looking for strays and got caught in a storm. He and Harris put the place together when Adam was a kid—some kind of Boy Scout thing, I think. They even camped out here once or twice, before Harris's health worsened."

"But if it was here—if all the time you knew—" She could only back away, staring at him in disbelief. Why hadn't he come for her? Why hadn't anyone come? How could he have loved her and left her here?

"I didn't know *you* were here, Marissa." His hands on her arms compelled her to listen. "To get back to the ranch you'd have to walk out the opposite way we came in today. It's pretty rough terrain, through dense bush, rocks, nettles. Even snakes. There is no path. It would be a simple matter to get lost back here." He stared at the small compound, shaking his head.

"I never imagined, never dreamed anyone would come here. In fact, I haven't thought of the place in years. It's too inaccessible."

Apparently it wasn't.

Marissa wanted to believe he was telling the truth. She wanted to cling to the faith Miss Blessing had encouraged her to rely on. But in some corner of her mind, a flicker of doubt surfaced. Maybe she'd been wrong to trust him? Maybe he—

"The smoke from the fires," she blurted out. "There must have been fires for cooking in that pit. Wouldn't you have seen the smoke from them?"

"I'd like the answer to that one myself." The sheriff rocked back on his heels, his eyes narrowing as they settled on Gray.

Gray shook his head.

"I know what you're thinking, Sheriff. But nobody would have seen smoke from a little fire. Not unless it was very thick and persistent, like a forest fire." He concentrated on Marissa. "You have to climb up a fairly steep rise to get out of here, honey. I'm fairly sure most of the smoke would have dissipated long before it could rise above that cliff." He pointed, held out the binoculars, waited while she looked. "We're in the backwoods, remember."

"But Cody made it to the church. How could that be?"

"I don't know. I wish I did." He looked at her helplessly. "I know our land doesn't go that far out, not all the way to town. But I've never tried to walk my way through. Years ago Harris got tired of losing animals back here and we fenced it off. Far as I know, no one comes in here at all."

"The abductor could have come out the same way we came in. If this was the place they were held." The sheriff didn't look convinced. "I expected to find some personal effects, cooking utensils, something. This place has been stripped."

"Stands to reason, Sheriff." The deputy glanced at Marissa. "Once she and the boy were out, he'd leave, wouldn't he? Relocate? Wouldn't stick around in case she led us back here."

Except *he,* whoever he was, hadn't taken off. He was still around, leaving his threats. And he'd left the picture. Marissa cleared her throat.

"Perhaps I should have said something earlier." That was an understatement. Gray would be furious. She glanced at Cody, who stood at the water's edge skipping stones, and lowered her voice. "When I was making breakfast this morning I found a gift I had wrapped and tucked away, ready to give to Cody for his birthday."

"You remembered his birth date?" Gray's eyebrows rose.

She shook her head.

"Miss Blessing told me it was coming up. I bought him a remote control car and hid it in the pantry under the bottom shelf. I didn't think he'd go in there."

"What's your point, Mrs. McGonigle?" The sheriff tilted his head back, his manner suggesting he was tired of the whole thing.

"I was trying to tell you. The paper was torn off and the car was smashed to bits." She took one look at her husband's stormy gaze and hurried on. "Some things in the pantry were out of place, too. I know because I couldn't sleep last night, so I straightened in the kitchen for a while. Mrs. Biddle isn't as fussy as I am, I guess. She just loads the shelves up willy-nilly. I like organization. This morning a lot of what I'd organized had been moved.''

The sheriff whistled his frustration.

''So now you've touched everything and we've no chance to get fingerprints. Wonderful!''

Marissa spoke to him, but appealed to Gray.

''I didn't do it on purpose. I'd already straightened the shelves before I found the gift. I thought perhaps Gray had been looking for something and had accidentally stepped on it—anyway, I didn't notice the car until it was too late and I'd touched everything. I'm sorry.''

''Believe me, Mrs. McGonigle, so am I.'' He snapped his fingers. ''Let's go, boys. There's nothing here that we haven't already seen, and our star witness doesn't remember the place.''

Feeling like a first-class idiot, Marissa stood watching as all but two of the sheriff's men mounted their bikes and took off on the same trail they'd followed here. The others conferred with Gray for several minutes, then set out in the opposite direction.

''They're going to see if there's some kind of trail that ends up behind the church,'' he told her.

She nodded and climbed on the bike, afraid to look at him lest he see the doubts that consumed her.

''I didn't know you were here, Marissa. Do you think I'd have left you and Cody here if I'd known?''

No, that didn't make sense. Whatever their feelings for each other, Gray clearly loved Cody.

''I know it's frustrating. It is for all of us. Nothing seems to make sense.'' He stood looking down at her. ''No one else but Adam knew about this place, Marissa.''

"Don't start that again!" She glared at him. "Adam did not do this and you know it. But I would like to find him, ask him if he ever had friends out here, find out who knew the place exists. Maybe Adam could help us find some answers. If only we knew where he was."

Gray wasted several minutes studying her. But he didn't answer, merely climbed on and revved the bike's engine while Cody climbed aboard. All the way back Marissa's brain repeated one line.

He knew. He knew. He knew.

The adult fellowship barbecue wasn't something Gray particularly wanted to attend that evening, but it had become a yearly custom for him to cook the steaks he provided. As things stood now, maybe an evening away from home with Marissa might help them both gain new perspective. Besides, he was loath to back out now and give the entire town of Blessing new fodder for their gossip mills.

If he got a chance, he intended to corner Luc and Joshua and pick their brains for some ideas about that cabin and who would have remembered it. Besides, maybe Marissa would forget their problems, if only for one night, if she got away from the ranch. Maybe she'd even lose that haunted look when she got chatting with the other ladies and forget about him and his accusations.

With Cody safely ensconced at the Darlings', under the baby-sitter's eagle eyes, Gray felt reasonably certain his son would be safe and not far away if help was needed. His two hired hands were staying on the ranch to finish some repairs on the barn, so he wasn't worried about trespassers. Especially not since the police were now running routine checks.

He'd taken every precaution he could think of to keep his family safe. Now if only he could get some answers to the questions that made his nights sleepless.

"Do I look all right? Is this what I'd usually wear?"

He turned to glance at his wife, mentally appreciating her slim body encased in snug blue jeans and a red turtleneck.

"You look...beautiful." She did, framed by the doorway, her hair a glossy fall of gold. Afternoons spent in the autumn sunshine, sketching, walking, riding, had lent her face a sun-kissed glow that helped ease the worried look he'd grown used to seeing flash through her eyes. She looked like the old, carefree Marissa. He bent, brushed his lips across hers. "You look perfect."

Marissa blinked her surprise. "Oh. Well, thanks."

He grinned at her shock. "You're welcome." He couldn't resist teasing. "You blushed like that the day I met you. Then you practically fell all over yourself trying to get into my arms."

"I did not!"

"Sure you did. I only came in for some doughnuts, and you showered me with a tray of chocolate chip cookies."

"If you hadn't stuck your foot out when I was trying to get past—" She stopped, stared at him.

"Yes?" He held his breath, waiting.

"I wouldn't have tripped," she finished on a whisper. "It was my first job away from home and I was so embarrassed that I refused to come out from behind the counter for a week."

He chuckled, pretended that she hadn't just recalled it.

"Blessing Bakery was never the same, that's for sure. Miss Winifred still claims that love cookie of hers got mixed up in the bunch by mistake, but I'm positive she put it there on purpose."

"I remember that cookie. *Don't be afraid of tomorrow. God has already been there.*"

He nodded, watching as the memories flickered back. He wanted to ask what else she remembered—their first date, their first kiss? Had any of the rest of their shared past made it through the stone wall of her mind?

"The next day you brought me daisies because you said they were like me—that most people bypassed the daisies for the roses, but if they only looked closely they'd realize a daisy could be wide open and still bloom. But roses bloomed, then faded." Her pupils dilated, the blue intense as a wash of emotions altered her stare. "You said I was the kind of person who went with the bumps, rode them through."

Her voice fell until it was a thready whisper.

"Later you said you loved me without fear because you knew I'd weather whatever life brought us."

He nodded, delighted to hear her repeat the words he'd said so long ago.

"The vows from our wedding ceremony. Do you remember when that was?"

She frowned, then shook her head. "No."

Gray swallowed his disappointment. She'd remembered much more than he'd expected. He should be content with that.

"Actually, our anniversary is the day after tomorrow. October tenth. Shall we go out for dinner to celebrate?''

He wished he could see into her brain, understand what caused that little furrow of confusion that marred her forehead.

''Anniversary dinner. Wait a minute. There's this picture I have, Gray. Of a restaurant. It's up in the mountains, and there's snow all around. Fresh snow. But inside, there's a fire burning. You're wearing a white turtleneck and a corduroy jacket. I have on a black dress that has little sparkles on it. There's a waiter and he's lighting a fire—''

''Cherries jubilee. I think you've ordered it every single year.''

''Yes.'' She was silent for a long time, her face pensive as she peered at him. The only sound in the house came from the ticking of Harris's clock on the mantel above the fireplace. He couldn't imagine what she was thinking, but whatever it was, it had her enmeshed.

The six bongs marking the hour broke the silence.

''We have to go, Rissa. I'm supposed to barbecue, remember?''

She nodded, glanced down at her shoes.

''I'm ready. Except for my feet. I feel like I should wear a pair of boots, but I didn't notice any in my room.''

''Sneakers are fine.'' He grabbed her fleece jacket, held it while she slid her arms into it.

''Yes. But this is a ranch. I know how to ride horses. Why don't I have a pair of riding boots?''

She wasn't going to let it go. Gray sighed.

''You do. I'll get them.'' He found the box buried

in the back of a cupboard in his office and dragged it out. The paper he'd chosen so carefully was tattered, its silver sheen tarnished. The big glittery bow lay smashed and ruined on top of the card, but he left it there, walked back to the kitchen.

"Here you are."

"What's this?" She accepted the box from him, and with a quick look at him, tore off the wrapping.

Immediately Gray was transported back to the last Christmas they'd shared together. Marissa loved the buildup, and she loved opening the gifts just as much. She was attacking this gift with as much abandon as then.

"Oh."

He watched her face, trying to decipher what she was thinking, feeling.

"They're beautiful. Thank you." She smoothed one hand against the supple red leather with its hand-tooled design, then lifted the boots from the box.

"They're your birthday gift. I had them made."

"My birthday?" she murmured, head cocked to one side as she leaned over to pull on the first boot. She looked at him. "In May?"

He nodded.

She straightened, stared down at her feet.

"They're beautiful. And they fit like a glove. Thank you so much." She wrapped her arms around him in a hug. "Now I feel like I belong on the ranch."

Since she'd embraced him voluntarily, Gray wasn't about to let her go. He drew her closer still, buried his face in the citrus fragrance of her shiny hair and held on.

"If I'd known that's all it took to make you feel at

home, I'd have given them to you in the hospital,'' he muttered, his senses zooming to life at the sweet seduction of holding his wife.

''Happy belated birthday, Rissa.'' He tilted his head and kissed her, allowing all the pent-up emotions of the past week to drain away as he relished the delight of her response. When he eventually pulled away, they were both breathing hard.

''Apparently there are some things you never forget,'' he teased, brushing a finger down her nose. ''Kissing becomes you.''

She blushed a rich rose and clapped both hands to her cheeks.

''I think this is where we came in.'' She giggled, edging away from him. ''I thought you were in a hurry.''

''Not *that* much of a hurry.'' He winked, then let her go, knowing she wasn't ready for more. Not yet. *But please God, soon?*

As they drove into town, it struck Gray that he'd actually prayed.

What was it that love cookie had said on that day so long ago? *Don't be afraid of tomorrow. God has already been there.*

The message was good. It was just that it was so hard to do. How could he not worry when a madman waited in the wings to make his next move?

For the first time in many months he wished he could just let go and rely on God to handle things. But wasn't that how he'd gotten into this mess in the first place—by not paying enough attention?

For the first time since the day she'd awakened in the hospital with her head pounding, Marissa found herself at ease in the presence of others. The people who attended the barbecue seemed like old friends. They greeted her, commented on her mile-high chocolate cake and teased her about her shiny new boots. Though she sometimes didn't understand what they were talking about, no one made her feel as if she were under a microscope, and no one asked about her memory.

"Nice boots," Dani Lawrence murmured, plopping down beside her while the men cleared the tables and handled the dishes. "Celebrating something?"

"My birthday. Gray bought them for me." She thrust out her foot and stared at her toe. "He had them stashed away in a closet somewhere, waiting until I came back."

"Hey, that's right. You missed your party!" Dani frowned. "Wish I'd known that. We could have done something tonight."

Marissa gulped, saw her turn and motion to Nicole Darling. "No, please. Don't!"

Dani laid a hand on her arm.

"Relax. I'm not going to tell everyone. Just thought maybe Nicole and I could get together with you for lunch or something." She waited until the doctor had joined them, then explained. "I'm planning a lunch date for us three. I know you're on call tomorrow night, Nicole. How about Sunday?"

"Uh, it's really nice of you and everything, but—" Marissa didn't know exactly how to tell them she had a date with her husband. How much of her private life should she share with these strangers who wanted to be friends? They were both recently married. They'd understand an anniversary dinner, wouldn't they?

"You're tied up?" Dani sighed. "And I can't remember what's on my calendar for next week, so I'd better give you a call. Is that okay?"

"It's very kind of you." Marissa wanted to confide in these women, but just how well did she know them? "Were we friends—before, I mean?" she asked hesitantly.

Nicole smiled.

"I like to think we were, though for the first few months I lived here, I'm not sure I thought about much other than work and Joshua." Her glance brushed over her husband, and her mouth softened. "I came as a temporary replacement for his partner, you see. And he didn't want me to stay."

Marissa leaned forward as Nicole explained the circumstances that had kept her from continuing the surgical residency she'd planned on pursuing.

"It's just as well God kept me here, really."

"God kept you here?" What did that mean?

"Well, that's what Winifred and I decided. It could only have been by His hand that things worked out so that I got to stay in Blessing, marry a man I love and respect and be a mother to three wonderful girls. Four, if everything goes well." She touched her stomach, a tiny smile flickering at the corners of her lips.

"I knew it. I just knew it!" Dani rose and hugged her. "When?" she demanded.

"Next spring, God willing."

"Congratulations," Marissa whispered. It must be wonderful to share that kind of news with those who cared about you, she thought. Then she remembered—

she must have done the same when she was expecting Cody. She glanced across the room at Gray and found his gaze fixed on her. Suddenly she felt cheated.

"Marissa, you're crying! What's wrong?" Nicole moved close enough to wrap one slim arm around her shoulders and hug her close. "I'm sorry if I made you feel bad—"

"Please, don't apologize for being happy." She rushed to explain. "I'm glad you're having a baby. And I wish you only the best. It's just…hard sometimes, not remembering." She lifted her head, noted that Gray was still watching, though now his silver-gray eyes had darkened to pewter. "Can I ask you two something?"

"Of course."

"When you knew me before, did you think I had a good marriage? Was I happy?"

"I was away at school for the past few years, Marissa, so I'm probably not the right person to ask." Dani frowned, shook her head. "And yet I am. Ever since you and Gray were married and you came to live on the ranch, I envied you two."

"Envied us?" Marissa stared. "Why?"

"You had it all. Anyone who looked at you could see it. You had some tough times with Adam, of course. And it didn't help when we had a couple of years of drought." She shrugged. "Life happened. But you two just hung on to each other and weathered your way through. I remember one Christmas—not this last one, but the one before. I'd come home from college dreaming about this guy I met. I was positive he was the one. You know?" She looked at the others, saw their nods.

''It was near the end of the Christmas Eve service. The pastor was reading the Christmas story and I was impatient. I wanted to get home and phone him.'' She closed her eyes as if picturing the event. ''I wanted to make sure that he didn't forget about me over the holidays, you see. Then I looked up and saw Gray put his arm around you. And it hit me. You didn't have to keep his attention on you. It was already there. You were an integral part of his life, and I suddenly realized that no matter what happened in your lives, he wouldn't ever forget you. You complete him, as he does you. I think it was then that I began to understand that was the kind of love I was looking for.'' She opened her eyes, grimaced. ''And it was exactly what I didn't find with the guy. But with Luc—''

She didn't have to say anything else. Marissa understood that Blessing's newest doctor took first place in Dani's heart, just as Joshua did for Nicole.

''Can I ask you something else?'' She paused only a moment, then poured out her heart. ''I believe Gray loved—loves me. And I think I loved him, too. But right now my feelings are all mixed up. Nothing is the way it was, nor is it the way I expected it to be. And I don't know if it will ever be the way I want.''

''I hear you. I remember that feeling so well.'' Dani smiled. ''But you already lived that past, Marissa. So what if you don't remember every detail? Maybe that's a blessing in disguise.'' She squeezed Marissa's hand. ''None of us gets to go back to the past. But we get today, and maybe tomorrow, and that's the real gift. You've got to do the best you can with them, because one day you'll be looking back at this time and the last thing you'll want is regrets.''

"She's right." Nicole looked wise even without her doctor's coat and stethoscope. "I had a professor at school whom I admired very much. When I was trying to decide on the next stage of study, he'd repeat a line that I've remembered ever since. Maybe it will help you, as it has helped me. This is what he said—far too many people spend their lives reading the menu instead of enjoying the banquet."

"You mean I should just forget whatever I can't remember and go on from here?" Marissa tried to understand how she could do that.

"You've already forgotten it," Nicole reminded her. "Why keep pushing yourself to bring it back? If God has plans for you to recall the past, you can be sure that He will arrange it. In His own time. Until then, all you can do is live today."

"Miss Blessing said much the same thing."

"She gives good advice." Nicole and Dani shared a smile.

"You know what's in your heart, Marissa. If you have feelings for Gray, then go with that. And keep praying that God will direct your path. Because He will." Dani made a face. "It might not be on your timetable, or in the way you expect, but He wants what's best for us. Always."

"Thank you for telling me that. It...helps."

"Now tell me about your painting. Have you done anything new?" Dani giggled at Marissa's surprise. "I know enough about you to know that those watercolors would draw you back no matter how badly your brain got bumped. What are you working on?"

"I've done a number of sketches of Cody." Not that anyone would notice, because they kept disappearing. Or she forgot where she'd put them. Or someone was taking them, as they'd taken the first. She decided not to mention it. "That's one thing my brain doesn't have to tell my fingers to do. They seem to know it instinctively."

"That's a good sign," Nicole reassured her. "Soon the past will be like that, too."

"I hope so."

The rest of the evening rushed past in a flurry of goofy games, funny songs and charades, which made Marissa feel very comfortable. After all, no one else knew the answers, either.

As Gray drove them home after they'd picked up Cody, she replayed the earlier conversation.

If you have feelings for Gray. She did. She had a lot of them.

The question was, how did she deal with them? She wanted to rebuild their marriage to what he'd led her to believe they'd shared, to relish the special times together, to learn how to relax and depend on him. But she was afraid, too. What if she never got back what she'd lost?

Don't be afraid of tomorrow. God has already been there.

The answer to her dilemma was clear. Whatever would happen tomorrow was an unknown. But either she met it standing strong and firm in the promises God had provided, or she stood shaking and fearful, in her own power. The choice was simple.

"Gray?" She took a deep breath, surprised by how right this decision felt.

"Yes?" He pulled into the yard and stopped the

truck in the driveway, his attention on something she couldn't see.

"I'd like to go out for dinner with you on our anniversary. Maybe we could make it a new start?"

His head jerked around, his silver eyes glittering like honed steel as they riveted on her.

"Do you mean it? Really?"

"Yes." She nodded. "I don't remember the past and I'm a little leery about the future, but I can't stay locked in this no-man's-land forever. It's time to move on, to make something of my life."

His hands moved like lightning, jamming the gearshift home, switching off the engine and reaching for her. Marissa willingly moved into his arms, her skin sensitive to his touch. His mouth closed over hers as if he were starved, his arms an iron circle she didn't want to leave.

"Thank God," he whispered when they finally broke apart. "Thank you for forgiving me. I promise you won't regret it." His lips grazed her ear, gently teasing its most sensitive curve.

"I had nothing to forgive, Gray. I can't even remember that day."

"Thank God for that, too," he whispered, kissing her again with a fierce passion that made her ache. Marissa shivered, relishing and yet slightly worried about the next step in their relationship.

Trust. That's what it all boiled down to. Trust in Gray, yes. But trust that God would keep her from making a mistake.

"What in the—" Gray eased away from her, his attention riveted on the farmhouse. "Stay here with Cody, but don't wake him up."

''Where are you going?'' She frowned when the dome light came on and she caught a glimpse of his hardened features. ''Gray, what's wrong?''

''Someone's inside the house, and I intend to find out who.''

She opened her mouth to protest, but he was gone, the click of the door latch the only sound to accompany Cody's soft snores from the back seat.

Marissa squinted into the darkness, saw a shadow move through the living room. Her heart began to race, her hands grew clammy, her eyes filled with tears.

''Oh, God,'' she whispered. ''Please keep Gray safe. Because I think I love him.''

As if in answer, a scream of terror rent the night air.

Chapter Twelve

"You didn't sleep again last night, did you? That's the second night in a row." Mrs. Biddle tut-tutted about the kitchen, like a mother hen with a recalcitrant chick. She filled a mug with fresh coffee, plopped in a dollop of cream, then handed it to Marissa. "I feel terrible for frightening you that way. If only I could have found the breaker box and turned the power on before you came home."

"It wasn't your fault. Gray says the lightning storms sometimes cause a surge that trips the power. We should have warned you about it." Marissa pushed back her mop of unruly curls and sipped the fragrant coffee. Maybe a jolt of caffeine would clear out the last fragment of her most recent nightmare.

"You're up already." Gray's voice behind her sounded gravelly, as if he, too, hadn't found rest. "I was hoping you'd sleep in."

"She hasn't slept a wink. When I got up, I found

her curled up in your office, staring at the sky. It's not good for a body to go without sleep."

"I'm sorry you couldn't rest." Gray squeezed her shoulder.

Marissa reached up to thread her fingers through his, needing the contact to drive away the nightmares that had plagued her.

"It's not your fault. It's the dreams. I just can't seem to stop them."

He bent and brushed his lips against her neck.

"What was it about this time?" he asked, pulling a chair close to hers, his eyes dark with concern.

"The same." She felt no embarrassment when his arm curled about her shoulders and he hugged her close. "That day the car went over. Watching it crash down into the ravine. The way he grabbed Cody and wouldn't let go. You know."

"I wish you'd woken me. I would have sat with you. We could have talked."

"There is no earthly reason that both of us should spend our nights staring at the stars." She already felt guilty for the time he spent with her instead of working. "I'm fine. Just tired. I'll take a nap later."

Gray pushed her hair back behind her ears, moved his lips a hairbreadth away.

"I might have enjoyed spending the night staring at the stars—with you."

Her cheeks burned at the wealth of feeling he injected into that whisper.

"You two remind me of my daughter and her husband. What a pair of lovebirds they were, always canoodling in the corners. It was so sad when he died." Mrs. Biddle set a plate with fluffy golden pancakes and crisp bacon in front of Gray. ''Broke my heart to watch her try to go on without him.''

''What happened to your son-in-law?'' Marissa asked, watching as Gray sampled his food.

''He was in the military. Died overseas. Friendly fire, they called it.'' She shook her head, her mouth pinched tight. ''Stupid name for sheer carelessness, if you ask me. That boy was brimming with life. He had plans for the future. Many times I've asked God why He had to go and leave Sylvia to raise her child alone.''

''It must have been very hard for her.'' Marissa couldn't imagine trying to raise Cody without Gray's solid support. A child was a labor of love, but he was still a labor.

''She had a lot of pluck, my Sylvia. She pulled herself together and got on with her life.'' Mrs. Biddle pulled a white handkerchief from her apron pocket and dabbed at her eyes. ''She and that sweet child were my life. I used to wish I'd died with them in that car crash.''

''I'm sorry, Mrs. Biddle.'' Marissa got up and hugged the older woman, wishing she'd never brought the subject up. ''Is that why you had to rush away? Something to do with Sylvia's affairs?''

Maybe talking about her daughter would help. As far as she knew, Mrs. Biddle's only friend in town was Winifred Blessing.

''No. I had to go see about Randall. He's—he's not well, either.''

''Can I help with something?'' Gray laid down his fork, watched as Marissa insisted Mrs. Biddle sit down and eat some of her own breakfast.

The older woman smiled through her tears.

''No, but thank you, Gray. I'm afraid nobody but God can help Randall now. He was so upset when Sylvia died, took it to heart. She was so good to him. He couldn't understand why she didn't come back to see him.'' She sipped a bit of the coffee. ''If only I hadn't gone in for the operation. I waited as long as I could. I thought he'd accepted things, gotten used to being without her. I didn't know—''

She burst into tears.

Marissa laid a hand on her shoulder. ''We've got lots of problems in this room,'' she murmured. ''And it seems as if on our own, we can't do a thing. But we can pray about them.''

Mrs. Biddle nodded, blew her nose and began clearing Gray's dishes.

''You're absolutely right, dear. I believe I'll phone Winifred and see if she can meet me for coffee this afternoon. You did say you'd made plans for dinner?''

''Yes, we're going out.'' Marissa smiled at Gray, her breath stopping at the look shining in his eyes. ''We have a sitter for Cody tonight. He should go to bed without a problem. He can hardly wait for his birthday party tomorrow.''

''He's a darling, that boy. Heals my heart just to see him smile.''

It would heal mine to hear him speak again, Marissa wanted to say. But she reminded herself that she had given things over to God. It would happen in His time, His way.

Gray pushed his chair back. ''I've got to get going. I want to get those strays rounded up before something else gets them. Adam phoned. Apparently he's been riding Dani's back forty and found a number of our brand in a gully over there. We're going to get them closer to home before winter hits."

"You're working together?" She could hardly believe it.

Gray rose, nodding.

"Looks like it. It's his idea. Says he's arranged some kind of payback plan to his creditors. I really think he means it this time." He thanked Mrs. Biddle for the meal, then turned back to Marissa, looping one arm over her shoulders. "What are you doing today?" he asked, drawing her along with him out of the kitchen and into the hall.

Marissa looked at him, and suddenly she knew exactly where she wanted to be.

"I think I'm going to help you round up strays after I get Cody ready for school. Can you wait for me?"

His answer took the form of a very satisfying kiss.

"Sweetheart, I will always wait for you. But if you could meet me in the south pasture in an hour, it would speed things up. I need to get the men organized. Besides, I want to come back here and spruce up for our night out." He winked, then laughed when her cheeks burned. "I love you. Did I tell you that?"

"Once or twice." Tonight, tonight she would say the same thing to him, when they were all alone and she could prove how much she wanted their marriage to grow strong.

"Don't forget it." He kissed her again. "I'd better get going. See you later, okay?"

Marissa nodded, watched him leave, then went up the stairs to Cody's room, her heart lighter than it had been since she'd first come here.

"You're already up!"

He grinned at her, his eyes sparkling just as Gray's did.

"Excited about your party?" She pointed to the bed and he helped her pull the covers into order. "How many people did you invite?"

He held up all ten fingers, then closed his hands and flashed them over and over.

"Cody, that's a hundred. You couldn't have invited a hundred people. How would we get them all in the house?"

He just grinned.

"You're a tease, you know that?" She swooped him up into her arms, planted a kiss on his cheek and hugged for all she was worth. "I love you, Cody McGonigle. Even if you are getting too big to carry."

She set him down, then chucked him under the chin with her fingers, loving the sound of his giggles.

"You like that, huh? How about here?" Cody was desperately ticklish, and when she moved her fingers behind his knees, he howled with laughter.

Finally he made his escape, tearing down the stairs and into the kitchen, where he hid behind Mrs. Biddle.

"Ha! You only think you're safe, little boy. Just you wait until tomorrow. Then I'm going to get you and tickle you silly." Marissa sank down at the table, watching as he crept out from behind Mrs. Biddle, sat down and began sampling his breakfast. "Daddy and I are going out tonight for dinner, but I got a sitter who will come here and stay with you. She's bringing pizza. Is that okay?"

He nodded, licked his lips, felt inside his pocket for

the little glass horse. Satisfied with its presence, he tucked it back and resumed eating.

"You'll probably fall asleep before we get here, but you'll be safe. Janice is a good baby-sitter. She'll have lots of things planned."

Cody set down his fork and looked at her with eyes too old for his five years. There was no way to know what was racing through his brain, but it didn't seem to worry him. Eventually he resumed eating.

"I could give him a ride to school, if you like, in my new car. It's about time I got back to normal and drove myself around, instead of asking poor Winifred to cart me around."

"You know Winifred loves it, but I'm sure Cody can't wait to take a ride in your car." Marissa nodded her permission and Mrs. Biddle began telling Cody all the features she'd requested.

Marissa waited until they'd left the house before racing upstairs to shower and change into a pair of faded blue jeans she found bundled into the back of the closet. They were a little tight. Perhaps that's why she'd thrown them away. A shirt, a warm fleece sweater and her boots were all she needed. She grabbed her jacket and tugged it on as she headed for the barns and Gray.

The crisp clarity of the October morning took her breath away. Here, in the freshening breeze, with bird-song drenching the air, she could hardly imagine that the terrors of her dreams from last night could ever become reality.

She hadn't told Gray the whole dream. The unspeakable part she'd kept quiet, but now it returned with all its clarity. She was back at the cabin, but she wasn't recalling the past. It was the future. Gray was calling to her from the woods, but no matter how she struggled, she couldn't get free of the bands of duct tape that bound her hands and knees.

A dark figure was leading Cody away from her, his cries filling her ears.

"Goodbye, Mommy. Goodbye. Goodbye."

"Marissa?" Gray touched her arm, causing her to jump. "What's wrong? I've called you three times."

"Uh, nothing." She couldn't tell him. Not now. It would ruin their day together and she didn't want that. Not this special day.

"But you're shaking." He pulled her close, wrapped her in the warmth of his arms. "Are you sure you're up to this? You haven't ridden all that much. Maybe—"

"Maybe I just wanted you to hold me." She shook her head, pulled away and tilted an eyebrow. "I'm going to help, Grayson. I need to get out of the house, into the sun and the fresh air. Maybe if I get tired enough, I'll sleep all night."

"Well, I hope not *all* night," he teased, but his eyes were absolutely serious. "If we get back in time, you can take a nap. How about that?"

She didn't want to go to sleep. Not if it meant another nightmare. But she pasted a smile on her face anyway.

"A nap? As if I'm some doddering old lady? I'll show you who needs a nap." She vaulted onto her horse and kicked it into a gallop.

No more shadows. No more clouds.

Time for a new beginning.

* * *

When the couple rode off, he stepped out from behind the toolshed and walked toward the house, searching the area for anyone who might see him and call out. He needed to talk to *her,* make her understand. But though he called and called, there was no one home.

Why wasn't she there? He needed her, especially now. He had to explain.

But the house was empty. He turned around, ready to leave, then decided to get a drink from the fridge. That's when he saw it.

A birthday cake. *She'd* made it, he knew she had. It was round with fluffy white icing, just like she always made.

But the name was wrong.

He wiped his finger through the blue icing, blurring the letters. That was no good. He hunted, found a knife and scraped away what was left. Then he made it smooth again. There was a little tube of colored icing on the counter, the kind he'd used to write his name on cookies a long time ago.

He picked it up. How did you write the name?

Sylvia was good at writing. She knew how to do it. But Sylvia was gone.

He stared at the cake, the pain in his chest getting bigger and bigger. Brett. He had to write "Brett." Then he remembered. A stick with two bumps, that's how it started.

Carefully he squeezed the tube so that it made a *B.* Another bump on crutches—*R.* A stick cut into three pieces made *E.* And then two sticks with tops on. He stared at his work. It wasn't as neat as the other one. But at least it was the right name.

He licked the icing off his finger and decided to come back tonight. Brett could have a piece of this cake, and then they'd leave. It would take a long time to get to the cabin. Brett would be tired. So would he.

He decided to lie down for a while. There was a big stack of fresh hay in the barn, up in the loft. It would make a good bed and no one would find him there. He checked first, then hurried out the door. Some men were working across the pasture, but they never even noticed him.

The hours of riding had taken their toll on Marissa. She didn't offer a single argument when Gray took away her half-eaten ham sandwich and ordered her to lie down.

"I won't sleep," she told him. "But if it will make you feel better, I'll lie here for a while."

He smirked but said nothing, pressing the edges of the afghan under her chin.

"I am not tired," she insisted.

"Forget it, Marissa. Stop arguing and go to sleep." He kissed her, then walked into the kitchen. "Any idea why there's a cake in the garbage can?" he asked.

"Mrs. Biddle is trying to outdo Winifred for Cody's birthday, I think. She must have made a mistake or something." Marissa yawned, but when Gray turned to stare at her, she pretended to cough.

"It looked all right when I saw it in the fridge last night."

"Gray, Cody will have a cake for his birthday. You

don't have to worry about it.'' This time she had to stick her head under the blanket to hide her jaw stretch.

''But why would she throw it out? I like cake. I could have had a piece.'' He took an apple from the fridge. ''Which reminds me—where is Mrs. Biddle? Wasn't she supposed to come back after she dropped Cody off at school?''

Marissa had to force her eyelids up to preserve her pretense at nonsleepiness.

''I think she did come back. The dishwasher has been turned on. Then she was going to see Winifred, remember?'' This time her yawn would not be smothered.

Gray snickered.

''I know, you're not tired. And I don't want to disturb you, so if you can stay awake long enough, I just have one more thing to say.''

She wanted to argue, but it was too much effort.

''Adam is meeting Cody's bus and bringing him here after he shows him what he got for his birthday. So don't worry about him. Okay?''

''Mm-hmm.'' She leaned her head back, allowed the pillow to take the weight of it from her shoulders.

''See you later, Sleeping Beauty.'' He touched his lips to hers, but she was already asleep.

Gray stood for several moments, content to simply watch her breathe. For the first time in a very long stretch he felt a wiggle of hope lift his spirits. Was this the fresh start he'd been hoping for?

He still had a hundred unanswered questions. But

maybe she was right. Maybe it was time to let go of the past and concentrate on today and tomorrow.

"I'm counting on You," he murmured when his glance rested on the old family Bible Marissa had been leafing through last night. "Please don't let anything happen to them."

Then he turned and walked out the door, choosing to ignore the persistent worry that would not be satisfied by the whisper of that simple prayer.

Chapter Thirteen

"Gray! Gray! Come here. Please, come here!"

He dropped what he was doing and raced for the house, his heart racing a thousand beats a second.

Adam followed two steps behind, muttering under his breath. "What now?"

What indeed? Only something urgent could make Marissa yell like that. The baby-sitter Adam had picked up twenty minutes ago stood in the doorway of the house, her face white with shock.

"She's in the study. I don't know what's wrong," she told them. "She just keeps yelling."

Gray brushed past her, half-afraid to face whatever this new test was. But in his study, Marissa sat on the sofa, still wrapped in the afghan he'd placed over her, Cody squeezed beside her.

"What's wrong?" He looked around, saw the windows still closed, with no signs of forced entry. "Are you hurt? Was it the dream again?"

"Oh, it was a dream, all right." She giggled, her

blue eyes dancing with joy. "A beauty of a dream. I remembered, Gray. I remembered!"

He gulped, tried to understand.

"Remembered what?" he murmured, taking hold of the hand she held out and sinking onto the sofa beside her. "I've been with the horses. I'm not very clean," he reminded her.

"Do you think I care about that?" She patted Cody's head, then let go of him to throw her arms around Gray's neck. "I remembered us. Me helping Miss Winifred in the bakery. You asking me out. The county fair." She pretended to frown. "Do you hear me? I remember it all. Even, you know, where you first kissed me—on the Ferris wheel!"

"Oh. That." He could feel his brother's stare right through his shirt and wished he knew how to get rid of him. Some things just weren't meant to be shared.

"Yes, that." She traced his bottom lip with her forefinger. "It was a pretty good kiss, considering I was scared of heights."

"I, um, I'll head back and clean up the barn, if everything's all right here." Adam grinned at Marissa. "I'm glad," he murmured.

"So am I, Adam."

"Want me to take a certain little pitcher with big ears along?" He glanced at his brother, snorted. "Never mind answering that. My daddy didn't raise any dummies. We'll be back later. Come on, Cody. I need some help."

Cody frowned, as if he didn't want to leave. But Marissa whispered something in his ear. He studied her, nodded, then finally left with Adam.

Once they were alone, Gray couldn't help touching

her, trailing a finger down her jawbone, winding his fingers through her curls.

"Tell me what else you remember," he whispered, steeling himself for the words that would explain her disappearance from his life.

"I remember moving here." She turned, glanced around the room. "I had a feeling that this old house would be a haven for us, a place that would weather whatever life brought us." Her gaze twined with his. "I remember wanting a baby so badly and wondering if we'd ever get pregnant."

"I remember trying," he whispered, thrilled by the flare of passion he saw fill her face.

"I remember going into labor." She grinned at him. "You were a little intense, as I recall."

Not even the embarrassing reminder of those hours when she'd been racked by pain and he'd demanded Joshua stop everything and let them go back to the way things were could wipe out his fear over what was coming.

"I remember Cody," she whispered. "Oh, boy, do I remember Cody." Teardrops welled, then dripped down her cheeks and dangled from her chin. "He was so little, so precious. How many nights did you spend walking him around in here until the colic finally left?"

"A lot." And he'd do it again, ten times over, if it meant he could keep them both safe.

"You love him. He knows that, Gray. He knew it even then. Remember his first word? Dad. Loud and clear. No mistaking that." She smiled, dashed away the wetness. "Oh, it feels good to remember those days."

"Anything else?" He had to ask it. He couldn't just sit here and wait to see if his world would come crashing down.

But Marissa was oblivious to his fears. She stared into the past, a half smile tugging at her mouth.

"Lots of other things. Anniversaries." She held his gaze, her own intense with secrets they'd shared. "This is number ten."

He nodded.

"I didn't get a gift! Oh, Gray. I'm sorry I forgot. I'm sorry my brain pushed all those happy days to the back."

"I don't want a gift now that I've got you. Anyway, it doesn't matter. It wasn't your fault." He drew her into his arms, breathed the sweet scent of her and knew it was the truth. Nothing mattered but this. "What matters is here, now, today. And tomorrow."

She hugged him, then rose, danced around the room.

"I can hardly wait to go out." She twirled a pirouette, then stopped, looked at him. "We are still going, aren't we? After all, it is our anniversary."

Yes, it was. But he was painfully aware that she hadn't said she loved him, that she hadn't whispered the words he longed to hear. Nor had she mentioned the abduction.

"Of course it's on. We're going to celebrate." He rose, held out a hand. "Sweetheart, do you remember anything about that day? Who took you, or why?"

She froze. Her face stilled, her eyes expanded to huge circles of black.

"No," she whispered at last, when his nerves were

stretched taut. ''I don't remember anything about that, Gray. Nothing.''

It was like watching one of her paintings get caught in a rainstorm. In the span of a few seconds everything was washed away. The joy, the animation, the excitement, all of it was gone. In its place doubts, fears. He hated that.

''It doesn't matter, Rissa,'' he whispered, gathering her close to shut out all the worries. ''It doesn't matter. We'll celebrate anyway.''

''Yes. I need to get ready.''

She shifted under his hands, and after a moment he let her go, watching as she climbed the stairs to her room—their room once.

Why hadn't he shut his mouth and waited until it all flooded back? Why had he pushed so hard?

Gray sank into his chair and stared at the blank computer screen.

Why?

The answer was painful to accept.

He wanted control of this situation. He wanted an end to the doubts and fears that it could happen again. Most of all, he wanted to get free of this feeling that he had to depend on someone else for his happiness.

From above he heard the sound of Marissa singing. It had been months since he'd heard her sweet voice. He froze, listening as the words to the song she'd been singing reached down and grabbed his heart.

One day at a time, sweet Jesus, that's all I'm asking from You.

But he wanted more than a day at a time, more than a few minutes meted out in parsimonious intervals with no guarantee that tomorrow would be better.

As he caught a glimpse of the cross-stitched sampler hanging on the wall, he was reminded of Harris's struggle to be freed from a life consumed by alcohol.

God grant me the serenity to accept the things I cannot change, the courage to change the things I can, and the wisdom to know the difference.

He couldn't change whether or not Marissa ever remembered everything. But he could change his attitude. He could stop waiting for the ax to fall and get on with loving her. He could do that.

Starting tonight.

Marissa leaned her head back against the seat and told herself to come back down to earth. But the dreamy quality of the evening did not abate.

"Did you enjoy the play?"

She turned to look at Gray, saw the flickers of silver in his sideburns. When had they turned color? And the fan of lines beside his eyes, was that from squinting into the sun, or from fretting over Cody's and her absence? How could she ever have forgotten this man and all he'd brought to her life? How could she tell him how much she wanted that life back?

"Marissa?"

"It was a great play and I enjoyed it very much. Thank you."

"Why so formal? And why are you way over there?"

"Ask and you'll receive." She unsnapped her seat belt and shifted to the middle seat.

"That's better." He looped his arm over her shoulder. "Had enough cherries for a while?"

"A long while." She giggled. "I never saw a waiter

so clumsy. I thought he'd set *himself* on fire before the cherries flamed.'' She lifted her hand, threaded her fingers through his. ''It was a great anniversary dinner. Thank you.''

''You're welcome.'' Gray slowed down, then pulled into a little picnic area off to one side. ''I have something for you.''

''Really? I forgot about this little habit of yours. Every year you take me by surprise.'' She waited as he pulled in under a lamppost, trying to stem her impatience. She had something for him, too, but the timing had to be perfect.

''I love you more now than I could have imagined ten years ago, Marissa. Maybe this will help remind you.'' He held out a narrow black velvet box. A fine gold chain twinkled on the velvet, a single star hanging from its center. In the middle of the star, one single stone glittered.

''My wishing star!'' she breathed, daring to touch it with one finger. ''I picked it out ages ago but I never expected you to buy it. It's way too expensive, Gray.''

''Then I guess I'd better take it back.'' He snapped the case closed and pretended to hide it away in his jacket pocket.

''You can't! It's mine.'' She leaned across him to free the box and found herself staring into his eyes. The time had come. ''I want it, Gray,'' she whispered. ''I want to wear it always. Because every time I look at that star I'll remember that tonight my dream came true. I love you very much. I want to be your wife, your partner, to be there for all the times we have left. I can't promise you it will be a perfect life, but I will promise to be here for as long as you need me.''

His hands moved to draw her closer and his lips hovered above hers.

"That will be a very long time, Marissa. Because I will always need you."

She looped her arms around his neck and drew his head down so his lips were mere inches from hers.

"Me, too," she whispered. Then she sealed the promise with a kiss that he couldn't possibly misunderstand.

They spent a long time in that picnic site, whispering the words all couples say to each other, reminders of the past, promises for the future.

But eventually, after he'd fastened the necklace and nibbled a sensitive spot beside it, Gray glanced at the clock on the dash and suggested they head home.

"*Home* is such a funny word, isn't it? Any place can be a home with the right people." Marissa laid her head on his shoulder and decided "home" was right here.

"It's odd, isn't it? A year ago I had so many plans for us, for the ranch, for the future. But tonight none of them matter compared to having my wife back."

"Ha! You say that now," she teased, half-embarrassed by her own eagerness to make their marriage complete. "Wait until I wake you up with one of my nightmares."

He raised one eyebrow. "I'm looking forward to it," he growled, a promise buried in his voice.

She blushed and he laughed, turning the car on the road toward home.

"Looks like all's quiet on the Western front," he murmured, peering through the dark to the house. The kitchen light cast a glow across the yard. "Everybody must be asleep.'' He leaned forward to glance along the dash. ''I guess Cody must have taken it out before we left.''

''Taken what?''

''His horse. He left it in here earlier.''

Immediately Marissa pictured the small glass figurine that Cody always kept close. Her heartbeat increased and a series of pictures, all including Cody and the horse, rippled through her mind.

''There's something about that horse,'' she murmured, rubbing one finger against her brow. ''I can't quite put it together, but I have a feeling that I've forgotten something important.''

''Like that's unusual.'' Gray smirked.

Marissa caught her breath on a prayer of thanksgiving. It was the first time he'd been able to joke about her ordeal and the aftermath. Maybe he really was ready to let go and let God. She whispered a prayer that this might be only the first step.

''Come on, Mrs. McGonigle. Let's go check on our son. Then I have plans for the rest of this evening. Lots of plans.''

''So do I.'' She slipped her hand into his, her senses zipping into overdrive at the blaze of love and tenderness that filled his face. They could make this marriage work. It was time to prove it.

''That's strange.'' Gray stood on the porch and listened, his forehead furrowed in a frown. ''I don't hear the TV. Janice loves watching those old movies you collected.''

''Maybe she fell asleep.''

''It's not that late.'' He pulled the door open, waited for her to precede him inside. ''We're home, Janice.''

But the sitter didn't come running out from the other room. In fact, there was no sound at all in the big farmhouse.

"What on earth. Here's a note. It's from Mrs. Biddle." He glanced at the words, frowned, looked again.

As Marissa watched, the same old fear that had been her nemesis for the past few months took hold once more.

"Gray? What's wrong?"

"I don't know." He lifted the note, looked underneath it. "She says there's a problem with her son, that if he comes here, we should keep him and call the police. She's left a picture."

"The police?" Marissa ignored the papers he held. Instead she raced up the stairs, straight to Cody's room. The covers were rumpled, but no little boy lay beneath them. Toys littered the room. But the little glass horse was nowhere to be seen. "Gray?"

"I'm here." His hands on her shoulders tightened. "He's gone, isn't he?"

She nodded.

"But where? With whom?" His hoarse voice reached out and squeezed her heart. "Who would take our son?"

"Call the police," she whispered. "Hurry." She heard him thundering down the stairs while she scoured the rest of the upstairs rooms. There was nothing that would explain Cody's absence, no ransom note, no explanation. Fear clawed at her. It had to be the same person, and he'd been inside her house. Again.

In the kitchen Gray was on the phone, his face white with fear.

"I don't know. We came home and he's gone. The baby-sitter's gone, too."

Marissa forced herself to pray. When she opened her eyes, she saw a piece of paper lying under the table. She bent, pulled it out. Sprawled letters in red crayon made her blood freeze.

"Daddy help."

"Gray?" When he didn't respond, she said it louder. "Gray!"

"I'm here—oh, my God!" The whisper for help oozed out of him as he stared at the printed words.

Marissa grabbed his arm.

"I taught him to write that. When we were at the cabin. I thought that if he ever let us out, if we got in public, then maybe he could alert someone." She licked her dry lips. "I told him it was our special emergency signal, like calling 911. Cody's in trouble, Gray."

He gazed at her, looking as shattered as she felt.

"Why?" he demanded. "I trusted, I believed. I relied on God to take care of my son. And now He's betrayed me again."

"No!" Marissa searched for the words that would reassure him that God was still in control, but she was too afraid, too confused by the rush of images filling her brain to offer the comfort he needed.

"Is anyone home?" Miss Winifred pushed open the door and stepped inside, her hands full of packages. Her eyes widened. "Gray? Marissa, what's the matter?"

"Cody's gone." She held out the note.

"Oh, dear." Miss Winifred glanced at the note, then slid the big white bakery box onto the counter. She set a smaller package down beside it, then took Marissa into her arms. "Have you contacted the police, dear?"

Marissa nodded.

Gray wasn't so timid.

"Yes, I've just spoken to them. Someone's coming, but I doubt there's much they can do." He glared at Winifred. "I did what you said. I trusted that God would take care of my son. And now Cody's missing. So what's next, Miss Blessing? Do you think God is going to bring him back to me? Do you think God cares that Cody is being terrorized by this person?"

"Gray, please. It's not her fault."

Neither Gray nor Winifred paid Marissa any attention.

Winifred met his accusations head-on, refusing to back down under his blazing anger. Her voice was firm, level, assured.

"God cares, Grayson. Whether you know it or not, whether you are willing to accept it or not changes nothing. God is the same loving father He's always been. He cares for Cody more than you do."

"Yeah? Then why doesn't He do something? Why doesn't He stop this?"

Shocked by his rage, yet understanding his fear, Marissa could only stand by and listen. But Miss Winifred had no such inhibitions. She shook her head, adamant in denial, before stepping forward and grasping his arm.

"How do you know He's not?" she demanded, her voice strident in the silent room. "How do you know our loving God hasn't put your son in a place where nothing can harm him? How do you know God's plans and hopes and dreams for that little boy don't go far beyond what you can even imagine?"

Gray stared at her. Watching him, Marissa felt some of his torture ease as he pondered her searching questions. She saw a flicker of hope.

"Cody was a gift to you, Grayson McGonigle. A gift from God who loved him, long before you ever gave that child a thought. He watched over that precious baby while he grew inside Marissa. The Bible says God knit together Cody's bones and sinew. Compared to God's love for that little boy, yours is nothing."

"But what if..."

Miss Blessing sniffed.

"What if the moon falls down and hits me on the head? You're looking through a keyhole, Grayson. And you've become so narrow-minded, so afraid to trust, that you're looking with both eyes. You refuse to see what is in front of your face, because your vision is so narrow."

"See what?" He lifted a hand, waved around the room. "I don't see my son, Winifred. How can I trust when each time I let my guard down, something like this happens?"

"*Your guard.* Don't you see? That's the whole problem here." Her voice softened yet became stronger, more impassioned. "You can't care for Cody, Gray. Not always, for every moment. Life happens, like tonight. So here you are. You have no clout, no strength and no insight in this situation. You're powerless. Your child is at risk."

Marissa watched his hands clench so tightly she was afraid. But Miss Blessing pressed on.

''Face it. The only thing you can do for your son right now is ask God to sort it all out. This is your crisis of faith—your future depends on the road you take now. This may be the very lesson God's been trying so hard to teach you these past months. Perhaps you are the reason He allowed Marissa and Cody to be taken.''

''Me?'' He stared at her aghast, but the words were sinking in.

''So now you choose, Gray. Choose to trust God, who has all the answers to any question you can imagine, or choose yourself. There cannot be two Lords in your life.''

Marissa stepped closer, forced his hand open so she could wrap hers in it.

''She's right, Gray, and you know it. We've done our best. Now this has happened. That doesn't mean we've been abandoned or forgotten by God. Now is exactly the time we have to put our faith in something beyond ourselves. We have to believe God has a reason and purpose for everything He allows, and we have to get our fears and worries out of the way so He can work it out.''

Marissa wanted to add something else, but Winifred caught her eye and shook her head. She was right. There was nothing they could do now, nothing except pray and wait for the police.

Gray was silent a long time. Finally he ran his hand through his hair. A faint smile tugged at his lips.

''Thanks, Rissa,'' he whispered, brushing his lips over her hair. ''It's good to have you back to remind me of what's important.'' He turned to Winifred. ''What made you so smart?'' he murmured.

Miss Winifred winked.

"History usually repeats itself," she told him. "But each time the price goes up. Let's just say I've paid, more than once." She took their hands in hers. "It's time to pray."

Because she didn't understand exactly what Miss Blessing meant, because she was worried sick about Cody and didn't know what else to do, because she realized the only answer to Cody's whereabouts lay in God's hands, Marissa bowed her head and listened as Gray asked God for a miracle.

The rumble of a motor broke the holy stillness they shared after Gray emptied his heart to God. Seconds later Adam burst through the door.

"I met the sheriff in town and he told me about Cody. He's rounding up a search party. Said for you to hang on until he gets here."

"Hang on for what? Has he got some idea of where Cody might be?"

"I don't know—he didn't share it with me if he has. But he did say not to touch anything in the house. That they want to get a good look, try for fingerprints."

"They won't find any. They never do. Besides, we've already searched the house. There's nothing here." Gray slumped, then remembered his decision to trust. "Let's get our stuff ready. They'll want to do a search of the grounds."

He pulled his jacket and Marissa's off the pegs. The bottom of his jacket brushed over the gift bag Miss Winifred had set on the table beside the cake.

"Oh, I forgot. A man stopped by the bakery, asked me to drop these off when I brought Cody's cake out."

She frowned. "I don't know how he knew about the cake."

Marissa barely heard her. Her entire body felt icy cold as she nudged the bag and the contents tumbled to the floor, landing atop Cody's note and the picture Mrs. Biddle had left.

"What in the world?" Miss Winifred knelt, brushed a finger over the tattered remnants of leather. "This looks like—"

"Moccasins. They're mine. Or they were." Marissa pointed to the picture. "He made them for me."

"Mrs. Biddle's son made you moccasins?" Gray frowned. "When?"

"That's Mrs. Biddle's son?" Miss Winifred stared at the photo. "But he's the one who brought that bag in."

Neither of them paid her any attention.

"When did he make these for you, Marissa?"

"When he kept us at the cabin. After I tried to run away for the third time, he became very angry and cut them up." She swallowed, closed her eyes, then opened them. "His name is Randall," she whispered. "I remember his name is Randall."

"Randall! Of course." Miss Winifred chewed on her bottom lip. "How stupid of me not to think of it before this."

"You know him?" Gray's eyes blazed.

"I knew him. Oh, it was many years ago. He was still quite small in those days, just a little older than Adam. His mother was the housekeeper here. Randall's father was abusive and she'd left him, tried to start again. It wasn't easy in those days. Harris felt sorry for the boy and included him whenever he could.''

''He called Cody Brett.'' Marissa held on to Gray as the memories flooded back. Days, weeks, months—they were all there. The fear, the wondering, the times she'd prayed to be rescued. ''If I insisted Randall call him Cody, he'd get very angry.''

''Brett was his nephew. I'm afraid my son adored him.'' Mrs. Biddle stepped over the threshold, her eyes brimming with tears. ''When Brett and his mother both died in that car crash, Randall wouldn't accept it. He went off his head, started acting strangely. He'd had mental problems before, but I'd always been able to calm him. This time he was inconsolable. I did my best to take care of him, but I couldn't move easily. I had to have that hip operation. So I did what the doctors suggested and put him in care.''

''I'm sure you did your best, Evelyn.'' Miss Winifred patted her shoulder.

''This is all well and fine,'' Gray muttered to Marissa. ''But I want to find our son.'' He cleared his throat, spoke louder. ''Would Randall have taken him back to the cabin? Did he even know it existed?''

Mrs. Biddle nodded.

''Oh, yes, he knew. When Adam's mother took him away that first summer that she and Harris had such a falling out, Randall became very upset. He persuaded me to allow him to camp out at the cabin. He knew it well.''

''But that was years ago!''

Marissa could see the tension stiffening Gray's broad shoulders. She felt it herself. It was a cold night.

Cody's jacket still hung by the door. Without that coat, he could suffer hypothermia. Or worse.

"Yes. It wasn't an easy hike, but Randall always thrived in the outdoors."

"You're thinking that's where he's gone? What guarantee do we have that he'd take him there again?" The sheriff had come in and now stood beside Mrs. Biddle, chewing on a piece of grass as he considered the possibilities.

"Yes, why? He must know we were there, looking around. Why would he go back?" Gray stared at each of them, silently demanding an answer.

"Because it was all he ever talked about with Brett. Staying at the cabin, having a campfire, watching the animals." Mrs. Biddle wiped her eyes, sniffed. "Randall wouldn't think about getting caught. He'd be thinking how much Brett would love to see the animals."

"She could be right." The sheriff looked at Gray. "It's your call. But if we spend all that time traipsing across country to that cabin and he's not there, we've lost the edge."

"I don't know what to tell you." Torn by the decision, Gray closed his eyes.

"Trust in Him. He'll lead you." Miss Winifred touched him on the shoulder. "'We are saved by trusting,'" she quoted. "'And trusting means getting something we don't yet have.' Romans 8:24."

Suddenly Marissa remembered something.

"Wait a minute. Gray, come upstairs."

They all trooped up, waiting at the door of Cody's room while Marissa pointed out the toys he'd left on the carpet.

"I thought he was just messy, hadn't put them away. But look closely, honey. Do you see it?"

On the floor the blocks were half-built into a small square house with trees all around. The builder had either given up or been prevented from finishing the house, but a blue sock was spread carefully on the floor, beside the house.

"He was trying to build the cabin," Gray whispered. "The sock is the river. Cody's telling us where to find him."

"Could be," the sheriff muttered, scratching his chin. "To leave clues like that, but—well, it could be."

"I got hold of the sitter, Gray." Adam peered in through the doorway. "She says a fellow turned up claiming he was Mrs. Biddle's son, that she'd sent him to watch Cody because you two were going to be late. She wasn't going to go, but he seemed to know his way around here and she'd seen him talking to Cody once before in town so she figured it was okay."

They all stared at Adam, shocked by his words.

"Randall wouldn't hurt him, I can guarantee that. Not unless you tried to take him away." Mrs. Biddle bit her lip, her eyes beseeching. "But it would be best if we went after him as soon as possible."

Marissa watched Gray's face and knew exactly what he was thinking. It was almost midnight, a cold, clear night without a cloud. Which meant the temperature would drop. There was already frost on the birdbath.

She took his hand, held on tight.

"Anything could happen," he whispered.

"They have the cabin. They'll have shelter."

"But if he builds too big a fire, or a wind comes up..."

"Don't think that way. God is there. He is watching, protecting."

"Think about the creek, Rissa. What if he tries to get away, falls in? He'll die."

"No, he won't. Cody is not going to die."

He stared at her. "How do you know that?"

"Because Cody won't try to get away. He loves Randall. That's why he never spoke in all these months. He was trying to protect him." She knew it was true as soon as the words left her mouth. "Sometimes, late at night, when I thought everyone was asleep, Randall would cry. You could barely hear him, but the sobs were so sad, heart wrenching. Cody would get up, go to him and hold him, and they'd rock back and forth. And Cody would tell him it would be all right."

"All right." Gray repeated the words in a whisper.

"Look, son, I know you want to go racing across country, and I would, too, if it was my boy. But we can't do that. As soon as it gets light, we'll start out. We can take the bikes partway, but we'll have to walk in the rest of the way." The sheriff looked at Mrs. Biddle. "I'm not risking him bolting."

Gray straightened. His fingers squeezed Marissa's hard, then relaxed.

"The morning will be fine, Sheriff. We'll be ready—you just let us know when. For now I think we'll go into my study and wait. We've got some praying to do." He held out a hand. "Miss Winifred, we'd be happy if you'd join us. And anyone else who feels like it."

The sheriff and his men left to organize things. Mrs. Biddle, Winifred and Marissa preceded Gray through the door. Only Adam stayed behind.

"Aren't you joining us?"

Adam stared at his half brother, his face pale, his eyes wide.

"I don't feel like I should," he admitted. "I've done everything I could to escape being part of this family. But I'd give anything if I could get Cody back, Gray. Anything."

"I know." Gray wrapped an arm around his shoulder, pulled him into the room. "But that's the thing about families, bro. Once you're in 'em, it's for life."

Adam cleared his throat. "I don't deserve this."

Winifred ruffled his hair.

"None of us deserves what we get, thank God. Instead, we get what God in His grace decides to give us. Let's pray."

Marissa closed her eyes, tried to keep her thoughts centered on God, but every so often they'd wander to that bare little cabin and the boy she loved beyond measure. Before she knew it, the tears were falling.

"Oh, honey, who's not trusting now?" Gray dabbed at her wet lashes. "Tomorrow's his birthday, Rissa. You just concentrate on throwing him the biggest party a kid ever had."

She met his stare, heard the unspoken words.

And pray he's alive to celebrate it.

Chapter Fourteen

"One of the boys found a little yellow toy up ahead." The sheriff's gaze held new respect. "That kid of yours is as smart as a whip. He's left a nice little trail for us to follow."

"But he hasn't dropped the horse."

For some reason Gray couldn't fathom Marissa seemed fixated on Cody's favorite toy.

"Good thing he hasn't. He might have cut himself on the glass." He looked at her, saw the bone-weary tiredness that bleached her skin of color and made her steps slow. "Are you okay? Can you hold up a little longer?"

"I'm fine. Keep going. We have to get to him."

"We will," he assured her.

They'd made good progress with the bikes, but this laborious trek through the dense woods was tiring for everyone. They'd shed their heavier coats a while back, since the sun's warmth had begun to heat the air.

"We'll find Cody," he repeated.

Marissa didn't respond, which wasn't much different from the rest of the morning. Something was on her mind, but she refused to share. Gray figured it was probably the sudden rush of memories that she sorted through as she plodded along behind him, but he didn't like it that she hadn't spoken about whatever was bothering her. At the moment, however, he had little choice. He'd rather she walk than talk. Even an ounce of conserved strength might make a huge difference to her ability to keep going.

They pushed on for another hour, stopping only once for a drink and a short rest.

"Come and share my apple, Rissa," he begged. Finally she sank down beside him, watching as he pared it into quarters.

"He didn't hit me, Gray."

He blinked, stared at her.

"That day you found me. I didn't have the cut because Randall hit me. I was climbing up the ravine and I grabbed a branch to pull myself up. It must have been rotten or something, because it fell. I tried to duck, but I was so tired and he was behind me and I stepped the wrong way, lost my balance. It knocked me out. But Randall didn't hurt me."

He didn't want to argue with her. But the memory of that day he'd first seen her in the hospital was too fresh. Anger sliced through him.

"Rissa, you had marks around your wrists where he'd tied you up. That wasn't a dream—that was real. And illegal."

"I know, but he wasn't doing it to hurt me, just to keep me from leaving with Cody. He wanted Cody to stay and I was trying to take him away. I believe he saw me as a threat to his future with Cody. He loves him, Gray."

"That's what I'm counting on."

They finished the apple without further conversation. A pall had fallen over the group, an aura of worry. Moments later they were up and moving again.

"Miss Winifred will be praying," Marissa murmured when they stopped an hour later. "And Mrs. Biddle. She's as worried as we are."

"It can't be much farther from here." Gray glanced around. "You'd never know we'd been through here less than a week ago. The evergreens do a good job of concealing things."

He saw the understanding in her eyes. She knew he was babbling in an effort to prevent the fear from rising up.

"Okay, folks. We're not far away now. I want no further conversation. Bucky's spotted them on the other side of the river and I don't want to spook him."

Gray opened his mouth to ask about Cody, but the sheriff beat him with an answer.

"The boy looks fine."

"Thank God!"

They crept through the underbrush and lay down along a slight ridge. The vantage point was excellent. Gray could see Cody sitting next to a long-haired, bearded man who bore little resemblance to the picture Mrs. Biddle had given them. A small, lethal-looking knife strapped to the man's leg sent shivers up his spine.

Please don't let anything happen to him. He's my son, my only son. I don't want to lose him.

The poignancy of those words stabbed him to the heart. Hadn't another Father given His son, His only son? Hadn't He promised never to leave or forsake?

With a pang of awareness, Gray's mind cleared of all doubts. He was powerless to save this child if the man across the river decided to harm him. One step, one false move, and the knife he carried could end Cody's life.

But greater power than he possessed had kept that from happening. Over and over God had proven His tender care for this child by protecting him. Would He do any less now?

It's in Your hands. I surrender my son's life to Your care.

Though he didn't speak one word aloud, the release of those unspoken words washed over Gray like a cleansing wave of pure clear mountain springwater. For the first time since Cody had disappeared, Gray took his hands and mind off the situation and handed it over to God.

Someone was speaking.

With a jolt, Gray realized that it was Cody's voice, the same voice he'd last heard long months ago.

"My name is *Cody,* Randall. I'm not Brett, I'm Cody McGonigle."

"No!"

Gray watched with swelling pride as Cody put his arm around the man's shoulders.

"Yes, I am. I live with my mom and my dad at our house."

Randall's hair swung from side to side. "No, Brett," he insisted. "My Brett." Tears rolled down his cheeks. "My Brett."

"Brett went to heaven, Randall." Cody frowned. "Remember?"

"No, he didn't. Brett didn't go without me."

"He had to." Cody thought for a moment. "God told him he had to go. Brett didn't want to leave you here, but Mrs. Biddle told me he and his mom got hurt in a car accident. You don't want Brett to be in the hospital, do you, Randall?"

"My mom was in the hospital." Randall stopped, rubbed his forehead. "I think she stayed there."

"No, she didn't. She's at my house, remember? We can go see her if you want." He moved as if to rise, but Randall pulled him down again.

"No, Brett. We stay here. It's safe here. *She* can't take you away again."

Cody looked up at his captor, his eyes sad. "You mean my mom?" He shook his head. "She loves me. She doesn't want to hurt you, Randall. She didn't tell anybody about our hiding place, did she?"

"She took you away."

Cody nodded thoughtfully. "That's because she wanted me to see my daddy. We're a family, Randall, an' families live in the same house."

"I don't have a family."

The plaintive words stung Gray's ears. This poor soul had lost his only friend—his nephew, Brett, who'd loved him unconditionally. How could he blame him for loving Cody, a child who gave love freely?

"I gotta go home, Randall. But I can still visit you. We can play our games. My mom and dad like it when I have friends over. We could play duck, duck, goose in my yard."

"No!" Randall grabbed Cody, swung him up in his arms. "*She* won't let me. She's mad." He walked toward the river. "Don't want to play that game. We can play swimming."

The sheriff lifted his arm to motion his men to move in, but Gray stopped him, shook his head.

"They'll freeze if they go in that water," the sheriff mouthed.

"No, they won't." Gray closed his eyes. "Go on, Cody. You can do it."

His whisper was too soft to carry to his son, but somehow Cody knew he was there. He lifted his head, searched the other bank, then smiled.

"I can't go swimming, Randall. It's too cold. Besides, I have to go home. Today's my birthday. Want to come to my birthday party, Randall?" Cody touched his cheek, smiled into the sad eyes. "We're going to have a big cake with lots of candles. And treat bags—do you like treat bags?"

"I can have a birthday here." Randall looked around. "I can make a party."

"When it's your birthday, I'll come to your house. That's what friends do. They go to each other's houses and take presents. Where do you live Randall? Is it a nice house?"

Randall frowned, looked around, then shook his head. "I don't know," he whispered.

"Your mom knows where your house is. If we go to my house, we can ask her. I want to see your house, Randall. Can I fly Brett's kite if I'm very careful?"

At the mention of the kite, Randall's face changed. He set Cody on the ground, took his hand.

"First we'll play here. Then we'll go to my house

and you can fly the kite. It's red and yellow. Brett gave it to me for Christmas."

"I'm going to get you a Christmas present, too. What should I get?"

Randall pointed to the horse clutched in his hand.

"You want a horse like mine?" He held it out. "It's not as much fun as riding a real horse. Do you want to do that later? We have lots of horses at my house. Here, you can play with this one if you want. My grandpa gave it to me."

"Fancy Dancer." Randall rubbed his finger over the mane. "Uncle Harris said he's a winner."

Gray felt the hard pinch of Marissa's fingernails into his arm. He twisted, saw her eyes blazing.

"That's it," she whispered. "That's Fancy Dancer. That's what I'd forgotten."

He didn't get it. The glass horse was pretty, a nice trinket, but he couldn't see how the thing could be worth the land Dermot DeWitt had traded it for.

But at the moment that didn't matter. What mattered was getting to Cody.

"I'm going to get him. Stay here until I motion for you." Gray stood, took a step forward.

"My daddy is coming, Randall." Cody's quiet reassurance barely broke the peace of the little glade. "I'll ask him if you can ride on the real horses we have at home. Okay?"

Randall nodded, but his attention was focused on the horse he held. Gray was able to make it to Cody's side before the man even noticed anyone else had arrived.

Gray reached out and lifted the sturdy figure of his

son into his arms and squeezed, trying not to show his emotions.

"Hey, Cody. What are you doing?" he asked when his emotions were finally under control.

"Me and Randall are playing." Cody's silver eyes were clear of fear. He even smiled. "Do you want to play with us, Daddy?"

"Well, I would. But it's getting late and the kids will be coming for your birthday party. Don't you think we should get home?"

"I guess." He pulled himself free of his father's arms, walked over to stand beside Randall.

It was hard to let him go, but Gray wasn't about to stop trusting now. They'd come this far. God would see them through the next stage, too.

"Hey, Randall, wanna come and have some of my birthday cake?"

"What kind of cake?"

"Chocolate." Marissa stood beside Gray, her eyes brimming with tears. "I know how much you like chocolate. It's your favorite. Remember how many s'mores we made? They were good."

"Yeah." He frowned at her. "But you can't take him. Brett's playing with me."

"I know he is. He loves playing with you." She walked over to stand beside him. "And I know that you love him, too. I know you would never hurt Cody."

"Never, never, never. He's my friend."

"I know he is. You're best friends. And today is your friend's birthday. You don't want him to miss his birthday, do you?"

"I made him a birthday." Randall pointed to a litter

of wooden cars, trucks, trains, all painstakingly carved from wood. "Those are his presents. From me."

"They're lovely gifts," she told him sincerely. "You were a very good friend to do that for Cody. He wants to have his friends visit him at his house on his birthday so they can play with his presents. Would you like to do that?"

Randall frowned.

"It's okay, Randall. Nobody's going to hurt you. We just want you to come to Cody's birthday party. Your mother is there. She's got ice cream and balloons and all kinds of things."

He moved away from her, walked over to Cody and took his hand.

"Can I ride a horse, Brett? Uncle Harris let me ride a horse once. I loved Uncle Harris, but he went away." His eyes filled with tears. "Everybody goes away. I don't like being alone."

Gray walked over and hugged the man he'd spent six months hating, his own sadness bubbling over as he remembered the pain he'd experienced without Marissa and Cody.

"I know exactly what you mean, Randall," he murmured. "I don't like being alone, either. That's why Cody's mom and I wanted him to come home. Because we didn't want to be alone. If you came with us, you wouldn't have to be alone out here. You could play with all the kids." He motioned the sheriff to stay where he was. "The only thing is, some of them are little kids. Their moms won't let them play with sharp knives."

Randall frowned at him. "Sharp knives are bad for little fingers," he agreed.

"Do you think I could look after your sharp knife while you played with the kids?"

"Well—" Randall removed the knife from its sheath, held it up so the light glinted off the blade. "It's my special carving knife. I made Brett's toys with it."

"Wow! You're very good at that. Could I try?" Gray held out his hand.

After a minute's consideration, Randall nodded. "But you gotta be careful." He watched as Gray whittled a hunk of wood. "Hey, you know how to do it, too." He seemed amazed by that. "Uncle Harris showed me how to do it. Who showed you?"

"Harris taught me, too. He was my dad." It was getting late. They had to get out of here before they were all forced to spend the night. "Want to go look at some pictures of him?"

Randall stared at him, shook his head, then moved back to Cody.

"No."

Gray's heart fell. He didn't want to hurt him, but what alternative would he have? "Randall, we—"

"I want to go to Brett's birthday." He grinned like a five-year-old. "I'm gonna blow out all his candles." He glanced down, noticed that he still held the glass horse. "Here, Brett. This is your birthday present. From Uncle Harris and me."

He thrust the horse toward Cody. But Cody wasn't quick enough. The entire group held their breath as the lovely glass figurine tumbled down and shattered on a granite boulder.

"I broke it! I shouldn't have done that. That's bad." Randall backed away, his face white with fear.

Marissa stepped forward.

''No, it isn't bad, Randall. It's very, very good.'' She bent over, picked up one of the hunks of glass. ''I didn't know this was Fancy Dancer. I'm glad you told us.''

Gray tried to see what she was looking at, but he wasn't close enough.

''Breaking stuff isn't good,'' Randal told her solemnly.

''It is if there's something inside that everyone's been looking for.'' She held up her palm. ''See what was inside Fancy Dancer?''

Gray caught his breath. In the center of her hand lay a glittering diamond, larger than any he'd ever seen. He picked it up, stared at it. Even Randall moved forward to take a look.

''What's that?''

''It's the prize, Randall. You found the prize.''

''Does that mean I'm the winner?''

Cody looked at his parents, then burst into laughter.

''Yes, you're the winner. Come on, Randall. Let's go have my birthday.'' Cody led him to the little footbridge and waited while he crossed. ''Come on, you guys,'' he called. ''I'm hungry.''

''You hear that?'' Gray tucked the big stone in his pocket, then draped an arm around Marissa's shoulders as they all turned and set out for home.

''Hear what?'' She frowned, looked around.

''The sound of our child. The sound of a miracle.''

She swung her hand in his, her smile wide.

''One of many, I think.''

''I don't understand—''

Her finger across his lips stopped the rest.

''Later,'' she whispered. ''At home.''

Chapter Fifteen

"This is the very best birthday I ever had," Cody mumbled, his cheek pressed against his father's shirt.

"It's certainly the latest." Gray helped him out of his jeans and T-shirt, into the cartoon pajamas he loved. "You better sleep in tomorrow morning," he warned.

"Uh-huh." Cody sat on the bed, watching his parents.

"What's wrong, son?"

"I was just wondering—what will happen to Randall now? He didn't mean to do anything bad. He just got sad inside when Brett and Sylvia and his mom didn't come and see him anymore. I didn't mind that he called me Brett."

"Didn't you?"

Cody shook his head.

"I knew who I was all the time. Cody McGonigle."

Marissa glanced at Gray. There was a lesson there

for both of them. Cody knew who he was because he had faith in his parents to fix whatever went wrong.

"Will Randall have to go to jail? I don't think he'd like it in jail, Daddy."

"I don't imagine he would. I think the police will understand that he didn't mean to do anything wrong. Randall isn't like other people, son."

Marissa watched him search for the words to explain, but Cody beat him to it.

"I know. He's big like a daddy, but sometimes he thinks like a kid. Is that why his mom took him back to stay at that special place?"

"He won't be there for long. She didn't know he'd run away, you see. She had an operation and she was in a special hospital for a while. When the people where Randall lived didn't get hold of her, she thought he was all right."

"But he wasn't. He doesn't like living there, Daddy. He's lonesome." Cody's eyes filled with tears. "He doesn't have anybody to play with in that place. Can't you help him, Daddy? Can't you do something to make Randall feel better?"

It was a lot to ask of a man who'd suffered for almost six months because of Randall's mistake. Marissa held her breath, watched to gauge Gray's reaction.

He smiled, ruffled Cody's hair.

"I've already done something. Dr. Luc is checking into some places that are nearer Blessing to see if he can move in. Then we can go and visit Randall. Would you like that?"

"Yes!" Cody threw his arms around his father's neck and hugged him. "Thank you, Daddy. Now I can go and play with him lots and lots. I want to fly Brett's kite.''

''So are you ready for bed now?'' Gray asked, tucking the quilt around the little boy's shoulders. Cody's eyes clung to his, the questions evident.

''Why did you do it, Daddy? Weren't you mad anymore? Did you forgive Randall like Miss Blessing said God wants you to?''

''Yeah, I guess I did.'' Gray turned to glance at Marissa. She felt the warmth of his love drawing her closer and stepped forward to take his hand. ''I forgave him, but I asked Luc to help him because of some other reasons, too.''

''What reasons?'' Cody yawned, didn't protest when Gray eased him down against the pillows.

''Well, number one, Randall loves you. I couldn't hate anybody who loves you, because I love you, too. Number two, because he took such good care of you at the cabin.''

''Yeah.'' Cody smiled. His eyelids fluttered. ''Good night, Daddy. Night, Mom.''

''And number three,'' Gray murmured, easing himself up from the bed, ''was because he helped us figure out a puzzle that's caused a lot of problems in this family.'' He stood where he was, gazing at the child he'd gladly have given his life for. When Cody's chest moved rhythmically up and down and his eyelids remained closed, he took Marissa's hand and led her from the room.

''It's been a very long day,'' he murmured, pulling Cody's door closed. ''I'll understand if you'd prefer to wait.''

''We can't talk here—we'll wake him up.'' Marissa

motioned for him to follow her into her room. ''Now, I thought we had something to celebrate?'' she murmured, loving the way his eyes darkened until they glowed. ''Are you saying you're too tired?''

''No, but—''

''Because if you remember, I had a nap this afternoon.'' She lifted her arms, stretched them around his neck and feathered his nape hair between her fingers. ''I'm not the least bit tired.'' She rose on her tiptoes, nibbled on his earlobe.

''But you had a very long hike, then put on a birthday party—''

''And the one thing that got me through it all was remembering that we'd be together, here, alone.''

She knew the exact instant Gray gave up trying to be noble and gave in to the love that had sustained them for ten long years. He sighed, his breath shifting the tendrils that drooped against her cheek. His head drooped until his lips were against her brow. Then his arms circled her waist and drew her against his warmth, into the cloak of his love.

''I love you, Marissa McGonigle. I will always and forever love only you. You are my life.''

She tilted his head up so she could see into his eyes, make him hear what she had to say.

''I love you, Grayson McGonigle, my husband, my friend. My brain blanked out for a while, but my heart always knew you'd be there, waiting for me. You are the one I want to live with, love and share all my tomorrows with. You are the only one who fills my dreams—'' She stopped, covered her mouth with her hand. ''Oops!''

He frowned, stared.

"Marissa, what are—you're laughing!" he accused.

She nodded.

"Why?"

"The thing is, these days I'm never quite sure what will fill my dreams. But it is you I love, Gray. I promise." She tilted her head to one side, watched him absorb that. "Can I ask you something?"

"Anything."

"Would you please kiss me?"

And he did.

Epilogue

July, the following year

Gray shoved the screen door open, tossed his hat on the stand and yelled.

"Marissa? One of the hands said you needed to see me."

When she didn't answer, he frowned, glanced around her immaculate kitchen. A pineapple upside-down cake sat cooling on the counter, and he was about to cut himself a hunk when he saw the note.

It didn't look like her handwriting. He picked it up, his heart pausing, then racing as the words sank in.

"Come to the meadow right away."

She'd been to the specialist today, about the fainting spells that had plagued her since the flashbacks had stopped a few weeks ago. She called them reminders of what God had done, but Gray knew she'd often kept the terror of those dreams to herself, trying to protect him. Was this about that? Had they found something wrong?

He grabbed his hat, raced out the door and vaulted onto his horse. He was halfway to the meadow before he remembered the verse.

We are saved by trusting. And trusting means looking forward to getting something we don't yet have—for a man who already has something doesn't need to hope and trust that he will get it. But if we must keep trusting God for something that hasn't happened yet, it teaches us to wait patiently and confidently.

He slowed the big stallion to a canter. The lesson had been well learned.

"Whatever it is, Lord, I'll trust in You."

He saw her as soon as he reached the rise of the hill. She sat in the middle of her daisy meadow, waiting for him, wheat-gold hair tossing in the breeze. She watched him ride toward her, the rich blue of her eyes a perfect match for the backdrop of the sky behind her.

He dismounted, saw the tears on her cheeks and whispered another prayer.

"Honey? Rissa, are you okay?" He dropped onto the quilt beside her, pulled her into his arms. "What's wrong?" He looked around. "Is it Cody?"

She shook her head, then drew back, away from him.

"Cody's fine. I'm fine. You're fine."

"Then what—"

"The baby's fine."

"The ba—" He blinked, checked her eyes now brimming with tears.

"We're going to have a baby, Gray. My fainting

wasn't because of any bad dreams. I've been rushing around too much and our child doesn't like it. I'm pregnant, Gray."

It teaches us to wait patiently and confidently.

"Didn't you hear me?" She looked worried now.

Gray leaned over, kissed her.

"I heard," he whispered. "I was just saying thank you."

"Oh." She moved into his arms, fluttered her lashes. "Don't you have anything to say to me?"

"That cake you left was delicious," he whispered, touching his lips to her nose.

"Gray! That's supposed to go to the Blessing picnic tomorrow." She lifted a hand to his cheek, brushed her thumb against his mouth. "Miss Blessing stopped me on the way out of the doctor's office. She really must get her messages from heaven, because she congratulated me and I didn't tell her a thing."

She stopped, thought about that for a moment, then remembered.

"She sent something. She said we're to open it together."

She set the little white Blessing Bakery box in front of him, laid her hand on his and together they lifted the lid.

"It's more of her advice, I suppose," he muttered, watching as Marissa lifted away the parchment.

"It's a love cookie. She told me she heard the words this morning while she was drinking her coffee. Look!"

Sure enough, the perfect golden heart sat nestled in the box, with red icing script across its surface.

You never know when life's greatest joys are sent as blessings in disguise.

''From God's mouth to Winifred Blessing's ear,'' Gray agreed, and proceeded to celebrate his own blessings with his beloved wife.

Dear Reader,

Welcome back to Blessing, a little town where life's difficulties turn into gifts. I hope you've enjoyed Gray and Marissa's journey to trust. It's not an easy one, nor fast. And some of us make that journey many times over before we learn that God is good always and forever. But the lesson is a valuable one that we can hang on to and that will see us through the worst that life can throw our way.

In this season of summer, I wish for you rest and rejuvenation, joyous memories to cherish and peace that will sustain you. But most of all I wish you love—oceans of it from the Father of love to your heart.

Blessings to you my friends.

Love,

Lois Richer

P.S. I'd love to hear from you. Reach me at loisricher@yahoo.com.